DREAMER

D1601425

Praise for Kris Bryant

EF5, novella in *Stranded Hearts*

"In *EF5* there is destruction and chaos but I adored it because I can't resist anything with a tornado in it. They fascinate me, and the way Alyssa and Emerson work together, even though Alyssa has no obligation to do so, means they have a life changing experience that only strengthens the instant attraction they shared."—*LESBIreviewed*

Home

"*Home* is a very sweet second-chance romance that will make you smile. It is an angst-less joy, perfect for a bad day."—*Hsinju's Lit Log*

Scent

"Oh, Kris Bryant. Once again you've given us a beautiful comfort read to help us escape all that 2020 has thrown at us. This series featuring the senses has been a pleasure to read…I think what makes Bryant's books so readable is the way she builds the reader's interest in her mains before allowing them to interact. This is a sweet and happy sigh kind of read. Perfect for these chilly winter nights when you want to escape the world and step into a caramel-infused world where HEAs really do come true."—*Late Night Lesbian Reads*

Lucky

"The characters—both main and secondary, including the furry ones—are wonderful (I loved coming across Piper and Shaylie from *Falling*), there's just the right amount of angst, and the sexy scenes are really hot. It's Kris Bryant, you guys, no surprise there."
—*Jude in the Stars*

"This book has everything you need for a sweet romance. The main characters are beautiful and easy to fall in love with, even with their little quirks and flaws. The settings (Vail and Denver, Colorado) are perfect for the story, and the romance itself is satisfying, with just enough angst to make the book interesting…This is the perfect novel to read on a warm, lazy summer day, and I recommend it to all romance lovers."—*Rainbow Reflections*

Goldie Winner *Temptation*

"This book has a great first line. I was hooked from the start. There was so much to like about this story, though. The interactions. The tension. The jealousy. I liked how Cassie falls for Brooke's son before she ever falls for Brooke. I love a good forbidden love story."—*Bookvark*

"This book is an emotional roller coaster that you're going to get swept away in. Let it happen…just bring the tissues and the vino and enjoy the ride."—*Les Rêveur*

"People who have read Ms. Bryant's erotica novella *Shameless* under the pseudonym of Brit Ryder know that this author can write intimacy well. This is more a romance than erotica, but the sex scenes are as varied and hot."—*LezReviewBooks*

Tinsel

"This story was the perfect length for this cute romance. What made this especially endearing were the relationships Jess has with her best friend, Mo, and her mother. You cannot go wrong by purchasing this cute little nugget. A really sweet romance with a cat playing cupid."—*Bookvark*

Falling

"This is a story you don't want to pass on. A fabulous read that you will have a hard time putting down. Maybe don't read it as you board your plane though. This is an easy 5 stars!"—*Romantic Reader Blog*

"This was a nice, romantic read. There is enough romantic tension to keep the plot moving, and I enjoyed the supporting characters' and their romance as much as the main plot."—*Kissing Backwards*

Goldie Winner *Listen*

"Ms. Bryant describes this soundscape with some exquisite metaphors, it's true what they say that music is everywhere. The whole book is beautifully written and makes the reader's heart go out to people suffering from anxiety or any sort of mental health issue."—*Lez Review Books*

"The main character's anxiety issues were well written and the romance is sweet and leaves you with a warm feeling at the end. Highly recommended reading."—*Kat Adams, Bookseller (QBD Books, Australia)*

"I was absolutely captivated by this book from start to finish. The two leads were adorable and I really connected with them and rooted for them…This is one of the best books I've read recently—I cannot praise it enough!"—*Melina Bickard, Librarian, Waterloo Library (UK)*

"This book floored me. I've read it three times since the book appeared on my Kindle…I just love it so much. I'm actually sitting here wondering how I'm going to convey my sheer awe factor but I will try my best. Kris Bryant won Les Rêveur book of the year 2018 and seriously this is a contender for 2019."—*Les Rêveur*

Against All Odds

"*Against All Odds* by Kris Bryant, Maggie Cummings, and M. Ullrich is an emotional and captivating story about being able to face a tragedy head-on and move on with your life, learning to appreciate the simple things we take for granted and finding love where you least expect it."—*Lesbian Review*

"I started reading the book trying to dissect the writing and ended up forgetting all about the fact that three people were involved in writing it because the story just grabbed me by the ears and dragged me along for the ride…[A] really great romantic suspense that manages both parts of the equation perfectly. This is a book you won't be able to put down."—*C-Spot Reviews*

Lammy Finalist *Jolt*

Jolt "is a magnificent love story. Two women hurt by their previous lovers and each in their own way trying to make sense out of life and times. When they meet at a gay- and lesbian-friendly summer camp, they both feel as if lightning has struck. This is so beautifully involving, I have already reread it twice. Amazing!"—*Rainbow Book Reviews*

Goldie Winner *Breakthrough*

"Looking for a fun and funny light read with hella cute animal antics and a smoking hot butch ranger? Look no further…In this well-written first-person narrative, Kris Bryant's characters are well developed, and their push/pull romance hits all the right beats, making it a delightful read just in time for beach reading."—*Writing While Distracted*

"It's hilariously funny, romantic, and oh so sexy…But it is the romance between Kennedy and Brynn that stole my heart. The passion and emotion in the love scenes surpassed anything Kris Bryant has written before. I loved it."—*Kitty Kat's Book Review Blog*

"Kris Bryant has written several enjoyable contemporary romances, and *Breakthrough* is no exception. It's interesting and clearly well-researched, giving us information about Alaska and issues like poaching and conservation in a way that's engaging and never comes across as an info dump. She also delivers her best character work to date, going deeper with Kennedy and Brynn than we've seen in previous stories. If you're a fan of Kris Bryant, you won't want to miss this book, and if you're a fan of romance in general, you'll want to pick it up, too."—*Lambda Literary*

Forget Me Not

"Told in the first person, from Grace's point of view, we are privy to Grace's inner musings and her vulnerabilities…Bryant crafts clever wording to infuse Grace with a sharp-witted personality, which clearly covers her insecurities…This story is filled with loving familial interactions, caring friends, romantic interludes, and tantalizing sex scenes. The dialogue, both among the characters and within Grace's head, is refreshing, original, and sometimes comical. *Forget Me Not* is a fresh perspective on a romantic theme, and an entertaining read."—*Lambda Literary Review*

Whirlwind Romance

"Ms. Bryant's descriptions were written with such passion and colorful detail that you could feel the tension and the excitement along with the characters."—*Inked Rainbow Reviews*

By the Author

Jolt

Whirlwind Romance

Just Say Yes: The Proposal

Taste

Forget Me Not

Touch

Breakthrough

Shameless
(writing as Brit Ryder)

Against All Odds
(with Maggie Cummings and M. Ullrich)

Listen

Falling

Tinsel

Temptation

Lucky

Home

Scent

Not Guilty (writing as Brit Ryder)

Always

Forever

EF5 (novella in Stranded Hearts)

Serendipity

Catch

Cherish

Dreamer

Visit us at www.boldstrokesbooks.com

DREAMER

by
Kris Bryant

2024

DREAMER

© 2024 By Kris Bryant. All Rights Reserved.

ISBN 13: 978-1-63679-378-8

This Trade Paperback Original Is Published By
Bold Strokes Books, Inc.
P.O. Box 249
Valley Falls, NY 12185

First Edition: January 2024

This is a work of fiction. Names, characters, places, and incidents are the product of the author's imagination or are used fictitiously. Any resemblance to actual persons, living or dead, business establishments, events, or locales is entirely coincidental.

This book, or parts thereof, may not be reproduced in any form without permission.

Credits

Editors: Ashley Tillman and Cindy Cresap
Production Design: Stacia Seaman
Cover Design by Deb B and Jeanine Henning

Acknowledgments

As most of you know, it's been a very hard year for me. I have quick ups and fast downs, and sometimes it's overwhelming. You have the family you're born into and the family you make along the way. I love both, and there's no way I could've made it the last twelve months without everyone's support.

I try to keep my stories slightly different from the norm—whether it's how they are told, how they are written, or just something unique about the storyline. Sometimes they're a hit, and sometimes I fail, but I always swing for the fences. *Dreamer* is a deviation from my normal arcs and conflicts. Writers try to push themselves because they want to give readers something fresh while improving the craft. This is that story for me. My friends have been extremely supportive in getting this idea to the page. I will forever remember Ana Hartnett's reaction to the story. It was exactly what I wanted. Thank you, Ana, for your honesty and just for being one of the most genuine people I've ever met. I'm so thankful to call you one of my besties. Rivs and Kerri—I love you both so much. You keep me laughing when everything else is a dumpster fire around me. A lot of my friends have been there to swoop in to lift me up and I will forever be grateful for your friendship and love. Nug MLM, BFF KB, HS, CW, Fiona, Dena, and so many others. I don't know where I'd be without Deb and Molly. Thank you both for your love and support.

Ash, thank you for pushing through this during a difficult time. I know how hard it's been. I appreciate your efforts and love you fiercely.

A special shout-out to my patrons. It was such a pleasure to meet so many of you in Denver. Vita! I love your daily affirmations to all writers. Every morning I look for your tweet because it's a great way to start my day. I'm sure other writers feel the same way, too. We did remarkable work in 2023! Every shelter was very appreciative of our efforts, and I will continue to do this as long as I can. Thank you for sticking with me.

And always—thank you, readers. It's a tough, competitive business out there, but you still buy my books and say great things about them. I can't do this without you.

To Kat J.
Because if I don't nail this…

CHAPTER ONE

"Go on a road trip, she said. It'll be fun. Thank you very much, Tamsyn. This is definitely not fun. More like a total nightmare."

I had twelve miles to find a charging station, and judging by the thick trees that loomed over the narrow road and no driveways in sight, I wasn't going to find one before my new electric car simply shut off. Quick flashes of light blinded me as the sun pierced through the web of tree branches. I slipped on my sunglasses and cracked my window in case I got stuck on the side of the road. It was noon in late June and the heat was beyond miserable. I checked my phone and held it up high to catch a bar, but there was no service in the middle of nowhere, Alabama. My anger rose as the available miles dropped into the single digits. I should've charged it at Target in Birmingham, but I wanted to get out of there as soon as possible. I wasn't the road trip kind of person, so I don't know why I let my best friend talk me into this harebrained idea.

"You need to unplug. You'll thank me for this." Tamsyn tapped the top of the car as though it was a horse and she was prompting it to get the journey started before rush hour in Shreveport picked up. I'd stopped by her place before my trip to pick up a cooler and whine some more about how I didn't want to go on this trip. I had zero desire to be by myself in a car for over eight hours. Most people loved driving as an escape, but not me.

That was valuable time that I could use to practice my upcoming speech or treat more animals. Tamsyn convinced me time away from my bitchy boss and bitchier colleagues was the best thing. She wasn't wrong, but I could've flown and been there by now.

Now I was four hours into my trip and I'd give anything for civilization. I almost let out a sob when I saw rooftops of a small town at the bottom of the hill I'd crested. I coasted down the road and breathed a sigh of relief that help was so close. Even if they didn't have charging stations, they would have cell service and I could call for a charge. That was one of the things I splurged on when I bought my eco-friendly fully-electric Chevrolet Climateer—a service package that came to me if I got stranded. Good luck finding me, I thought. As I coasted into town, I looked for a name welcoming me but found nothing. With two miles left on my DTE, distance-to-empty, I pulled over to park, misjudged the height of the curb, and scraped the underbelly on the sidewalk.

"Fuck!" This car was less than four months old and I was destroying it with bad decisions.

A cute woman with curly shoulder-length blond hair and wide hazel eyes approached me. "Are you okay?" She pointed to the car, and for a moment I wondered how she knew I needed a charge. "That was quite a scrape." So, she heard it, too.

"That was pretty loud, huh?" In my head, it sounded like a crash. I cringed and blew out my breath when she nodded. I opened the door and squatted next to her as though I knew, or even that she knew, what we were looking at.

"Nothing seems to be leaking," she said. Her voice was confident and made me believe maybe she did know something about cars even though the back tire and most of the underbelly were perched on the sidewalk.

I was too afraid to drive it off the edge of the cement just in case I caused further damage. "It's electric. I don't know if that makes a difference." I stood when she did.

She was attractive, maybe my age or a few years younger, and smelled like orange blossoms and fresh linen. The light blue summer dress with thick shoulder straps brought out the blue in her hazel eyes. Her wedge sandals gave her a few inches over me, but we were probably the same height if she were barefoot.

I looked around the town square, and I knew the answer before I even asked the question. "Are there any charging stations here in town?"

She shook her head apologetically. "I'm sorry. The closest big town is Harperville. They have Target and Walmart. I bet they have what you need. We don't even have a traffic signal." She waved her hand around her as though this was the whole town. "Also, hi. I'm Macey. I work up at the library." Her slight accent was adorable. It wasn't as pronounced or as sharp as Tamsyn's daughter Arya's, but there was no mistaking that she was from the south.

I remembered my manners and made a proper introduction before I full-on embraced the panic squeezing my chest. "Hi, Macey. I'm Sawyer. It's nice to meet you." I looked back at my car and felt more weight bear down on my shoulders. This wasn't good. "How far away is Harperville?" I knew full well I'd never make it there, but maybe the local Chevrolet dealership had a charging station they could bring out to me.

She shrugged. "Maybe twenty-five miles? It usually takes about forty minutes to get there."

"Thank you for your help. I'll just call the dealership and have somebody come out." I looked at the buildings for any cute signs or identification. "Where exactly am I?"

"You're in Ladybug Junction. I'd like to officially welcome you even though it isn't under better circumstances."

I waved her off as though this wasn't a big deal when I knew damn well that I just lost valuable time by being a dumbass. I grabbed my phone but couldn't get cell service. I held it up looking for bars, but I only saw the tiny words "no service" in the upper right-hand corner. "How do you not have service here?"

"Oh, we do. Up at the library." She pointed to a brick building up the hill a block away. "I'm headed there if you want to join me. I'm one of the librarians and can hook you up with our Wi-Fi. You can call the people you need to."

"I'd appreciate that. Thanks." I grabbed my messenger bag and followed her.

She wasn't shy and fed me bits and pieces of information about the town. "We have one school for grade school, middle school, and high school. It's the large white building down on Liberty Street. Some of the classes are held at the library, but since school is out, it's pretty quiet."

"How long have you lived here?" I asked. She looked fresh under the beating heat of the midday sun while I wilted and tried discreetly to wipe the pool of sweat that rested above my belt without drawing attention. I smoothed down the front of my shirt and waved the back loose to circulate the hot, humid heat away from my skin.

"My whole life. My great-great-grandparents helped build this town. My parents, aunts and uncles, and my three brothers still live here."

She unlocked the side door to the library and held it open for me. I was instantly appreciative of the cold air that enveloped me.

"I didn't realize how hot it was outside." Total lie, but our conversation had reached a lull and I wanted to contribute.

"It's a real scorcher. It's a good thing your car made it here," she said. She handed me a laminated instruction guide for internet and Wi-Fi use.

"How do you call people if there aren't any cell phone towers?" I asked.

She pointed to an office phone sitting on her desk. "We still have landlines. And hot spots. The library rents them out. Good news. We're supposed to get a cell tower this fall."

I was shocked that there were still pockets of small-town life where people didn't have internet everywhere. "Do you all have dial-up or something?" I asked. I liked the softness of her laugh and the way her curls bounced when she nodded. "It's a legitimate question, right?"

"Totally legitimate. Maybe some people do, but the library has cable with Wi-Fi. Go ahead and find a comfortable place to make your calls. I'll be over there if you need me." She pointed to a desk in the corner and smiled as she walked away.

I took a moment to appreciate the gentle sway of her hips and how her shoulders and back were void of any freckles. Her sun-kissed skin was flawless and a stark contrast to my paleness. It was a subtle reminder that I needed to get away from work and do something fun like hang out at Tamsyn's pool or go canoeing with my family. I sat at a table near the magazines and scrolled on my phone until I found the email from the dealership. Any dealership would be able to help me; I just needed to reference the warranty number.

"Sunlight Chevrolet. How may I help you?" The pleasant, stress-free voice irritated me.

"Hi, I'm Sawyer Noel. I purchased a Climateer a few months ago with the roadside assistance package. I'm going to need it."

"I'll connect you to our eco-friendly service department. Please hold." She practically sang it to me, which elevated my anxiety even more.

"Service Department. How can I help you?"

"This is Sawyer Noel. I'm stuck in a little town nearby called Ladybug Junction, Alabama, and I'm going to need a charge. I have an account with Chevrolet." I rattled off the warranty number and waited silently as he filled the void by loudly clicking the computer keys and breathed heavily through his mouth until he answered me.

"Okay, I see that you've purchased our roadside plan. Let me check the schedule and see how long it's going to take us to get to you. Please hold," he said.

I sighed and sank into the chair. I had days before the conference started, so this little setback wasn't going to hurt me.

"Ms. Noel? I found a technician close to you. He can be there in about three hours."

"Three hours?" My voice drew the attention of not only the two other patrons in the library, but Macey looked at me as well. I lowered my voice. "Three hours? I mean, the nearest town is less than an hour away."

"Do you have enough charge to get you there?" His nasal voice was overly annoying.

"No, or I would've done that." I pinched the bridge of my nose and closed my eyes to stop the tension headache that was beginning to poke my brain.

"To keep the warranty, one of our own technicians has to come out there to either charge or tow. Most tow truck drivers don't know the delicate underbelly of the Climateer. I'll have Stat Towing get in touch with you. They should be there by four. I'll have them call you to confirm."

"Tell them cell phone reception is sketchy, so leave a message if I don't answer." I hung up feeling only a little less overwhelmed. It was obvious I did damage underneath, but hopefully it was a quick fix.

Macey was immediately in my space when I hung up. "Three hours is a long time to wait. How about I buy you an iced tea from the diner at the corner? Or lunch if you're hungry."

"You heard I have time to kill, huh? I appreciate the offer, but I know you have work and better things to do," I said. Any other day, lunch with a beautiful woman would be wonderful, but I felt frumpy and unsettled and knew I would be terrible company. She persisted.

"Tilly makes the best cherry pie, and the diner's chicken salad on croissant is to die for," she said. She leaned closer to my face and pointed at my stomach. "Judging by that really loud rumble that was hard to ignore, I'm guessing lunch sounds good. And there's Wi-Fi at the diner, too, so you won't miss a call. Come on. I'll take my lunch break now."

Even though my situation felt overwhelming, I could feel my

resolve crumble. Macey was attractive and I liked the attention she gave me. My stomach rumbled again at the thought of cherry pie. "Okay, but can you give me a few minutes to freshen up?"

She smiled and pointed to the restrooms at the end of the hall. "I'll finish a few things and meet you back here in five. Is that good?"

I nodded. "Thank you."

I didn't look as frazzled as I felt. My cheeks were somewhat flushed, which made my dull blue eyes seem brighter. I chalked it up to my situation and the terrible heat and ignored that it might be because of Macey. I pulled my dark brown hair back in a bun and made sure the makeup I applied six hours ago hadn't melted in this godforsaken heat.

When I met Macey, she, too, had put her hair up. "I promise you won't be disappointed," she said. She gave some instructions to the other librarian before we slipped back out into the heat and walked the short distance to Tilly's Diner.

I fumbled for my sunglasses while wincing at the brightness. A different headache tapped at the back of my head, threatening to become worse unless I ate something. It had been hours since my oatmeal raisin breakfast bar. I needed carbs and something cold to drink.

"Is Tilly a real person?" I asked.

"Of course she is. It's her diner. She might be eighty years old, but she's a real spitfire."

"Does she still cook?" The idea of working past my sixties wasn't in my life plan. And I wasn't fond of cooking.

"She only bakes. Most days she knits in a booth near the kitchen and completely inserts herself in any conversation her hearing aids pick up."

"Hopefully, she'll find me boring."

Macey gave me a hard stare. "I doubt that very much."

A blush feathered across my cheeks and heat spread down my neck at her words. "No, I'm quite boring. Trust me, she'll ignore me."

The smell of hot greasy fries and cheeseburgers wafted in the cool air when I followed Macey inside the bustling diner.

"Hi, Uncle Fred." Macey walked straight into the outstretched arms of an older man with thick, graying eyebrows and a beard in need of trimming. He gave her a quick hug and a kiss on the cheek. She turned to introduce me. "This is my friend Sawyer. Sawyer, this is my uncle."

He promptly shook my hand. "Hello, Sawyer."

"Sawyer's stuck here for a bit, so I thought I'd bring her to the best diner in town," Macey said.

"Well, let's get you seated. I'll send Damon over to take your order. Welcome to Ladybug Junction," he said.

Macey pointed to a booth. I slid along the vinyl padded bench seat and settled in the middle. She sat directly across from me.

"Does your uncle run the place?" I asked.

"He's one of the managers here. Sometimes he cooks. He fills in whenever he's needed."

I unfolded the menu and looked at the lunch selection. "Do you still recommend the chicken salad and pie?"

"It's my favorite," she said.

"Then I'll take it."

I folded the menu without studying it and placed it at the end of the table. The diner was exactly what I pictured a small-town diner would look like. Fifties vibe, silver accents, and teal with glitter padded seats. Since it was after one, the lunch rush was trickling out.

"Hi, Macey and special guest. What can I get you two?" A waiter set two waters on the cracked Formica.

"Hi, Damon. This is Sawyer. We'd both like the chicken salad sandwich, iced teas, and cherry pie."

"The usual, then," he said. He swiped our menus off the table and hustled off.

My anxiety tiptoed in the empty space between us. I wanted to engage her, but I hadn't had to strike up a conversation with a stranger in a long time that didn't involve the treatment of an animal. "So, you've lived here your entire life. What's there to do for fun here?"

"Read." She volleyed the glass of ice water between her hands along the condensation that pooled around the base of the glass. Her trimmed, short nails were painted pale pink and a small heart tattoo rested on the inside of her left wrist.

"Says the town librarian. There has to be more to this town than reading. What do you and your friends do? What do you do when you're not working?"

She shrugged. "You wouldn't think so, but I work a lot. With only four employees, time off is hard to manage."

It was hard to believe that a small-town librarian was swamped, and I hated that I immediately assumed her job was unimportant. Maybe she had a ton of hobbies. Macey struck me as the kind of person who liked to stay busy. She probably volunteered at every dog shelter and nursing home in the tri-county area.

I wondered if she was single. The only jewelry I saw was a thin silver ring that circled her right middle finger with an engraving I couldn't read without cocking my head and blatantly staring. Her left hand was void of any rings. "Do you have a boyfriend? Girlfriend? Are there couples things to do around here?" I didn't want to assume her sexuality and I didn't want her to think that it was the only thing that I was interested in.

"No. There aren't a lot of prospects for me around here, but I do have a lot of friends. Sometimes I go canoeing with them if there's a long holiday weekend. Sometimes we just hang around and watch movies or grill out. Small-town life is for people who like to do things at their own pace."

That sounded wonderful. Tamsyn was my best friend and we did hang, but she was getting more and more involved in Arya's sports and dance classes, so finding time together was getting harder. "I work a lot, too."

"What do you do?"

"I'm a veterinarian. I'm on my way to a convention in Atlanta."

Macey lifted her eyebrow in surprise. "Wow. That's fantastic. It must be so great to work with animals."

"It is but I always get the broken bones, vomiting cats, and stressful emergency surgeries. I'd like a few more yearly exams and simple shots," I said.

"Yeah, that sounds scary. The people you work with must really trust you. How rewarding."

Guilt washed over me as I thought about how many times I complained to my boss, Oliver Strong, about the crappy visits I was handed, but maybe the techs thought I was better equipped to handle the more serious cases. I'd been so laser-focused on judging Meredith, one of the other veterinarians, and feeling left out, that the thought never crossed my mind until now. I worked twice as hard as my colleagues and much longer hours. When I voiced my concerns to Oliver he just laughed and waved me off, saying that nobody was playing favorites and I was overly sensitive. He strongly suggested I take the entire week to reflect and recenter.

"It's so rewarding that I'm thinking of opening up my own practice," I said.

Macey reached out and squeezed my fingers before quickly pulling away. "That's wonderful. Is that what the convention is about?" she asked.

"No. It's a continuing education seminar. We learn new things and we have guest speakers who discuss new medications and new techniques. I have a small speech, but it's not exciting." I tried to make it as vague as possible because I knew what I did was either boring to people or they didn't want to hear about hurt animals. "Do you have any pets?"

"I have a hedgehog."

"Oh, my goodness. How sweet! I've never treated a hedgehog before."

Macey smiled. "He's adorable and keeps me entertained.

He's the perfect companion. Squeaks when I walk into the room and grunts when he wants to play."

"He sounds amazing."

"He's a little prickly and headstrong, but we have a good relationship." She was so comfortable and confident in her skin. She only knew me for thirty minutes but treated me as if I was a close friend she'd known for years.

I wondered how many people lived in Ladybug Junction. Main Street had a barber, a coffee shop with a red-and-white porcelain sign, a cobbler, and Maryann's Must Haves. Those were the only shops I could see. I leaned closer to Macey. "Why ladybugs?"

"What do you mean?"

"The town name, the library, and all the kitschy things in the display windows. I'm surprised this restaurant isn't called Ladybug Diner."

"Ladybugs fly through this part of the country during their migration," she said. She briefly touched my hand. "Fifty years ago, this town was called Memorial Junction. Now, where's the fun in that name?"

"Do I even want to know why it was called Memorial Junction?"

"Alabama was active in the Civil War."

I held my hand up to stop her. "I get it. And ladybugs are more fun."

"The tourists are different. We used to do Civil War reenactments, but we voted to discontinue them. The wrong kind of people were visiting," she said. Macey leaned back when Damon slid two lunch plates in front of us. "And ask yourself who can hate ladybugs?"

This felt so unbelievable. A small town like this in the middle of nowhere with no cell reception and only glimpses of modern-day life was equal parts unnerving and relaxing. A part of me welcomed the peace, but the other, stronger part of me told me to run. I blamed Tamsyn and her love of scary movies. If I hadn't seen movies like *Get Out* or *Deliverance*, I would be completely at ease. Instead, I was rubbing the back of my neck and hoping this pretty woman in front of me couldn't tell I was sweating. "Well, it's a bug and I don't like them, so I'm the wrong person to ask."

She leaned forward and whispered, "You probably should keep that to yourself."

She looked so serious until she delivered the perfect wink. I felt the tension crack and fall off my shoulders in chunks. Even though I felt out of sorts with a broken-down car and a town full of strangers, I was grateful that Macey happened to run into me today.

Chapter Two

The shrill of the tow truck's backup alarm bounced off the buildings, amplifying the annoying continuous beep. I cringed as the driver took his time trying to figure out how to get my car off the curb without doing more damage. Macey gently pulled me away from the street.

"I'm sure he knows what he's doing, but let's give him some space just in case," she said. Her warm breath tickled the back of my neck, and my skin under her fingertips tingled as she guided me to stand a safe distance.

"I don't know what you got it stuck on, but it's not budging." The tow truck driver swept off his ballcap and slapped it across his knee to rid it of dust.

Both Macey and I took another step back. We watched him carefully jack the car up and off the curb before slipping the tow sling underneath.

"They definitely don't make cars like they used to," he said. I wasn't taking the bait. He squinted up at me and shook his head. "I have a '69 Camaro and a 1986 Ford F150. Both can handle a few bangs. And can handle curbs." He pointed to an obvious dent. "I'm never buying an electric car. Too delicate for me." He wiggled his fingers and raised his voice at the word "delicate."

I wasn't amused and he got the hint. He tucked his Insane Clown Posse sleeveless shirt into his jeans and turned his focus back on my car. After ten minutes of finagling it onto the bed of the tow truck, he handed me paperwork to sign.

"Do you want to ride into Harperville? The dealership closes in thirty, but I can give you a ride to a hotel close to them. There isn't a car rental place, but they might be able to give you a loaner. I don't work there so I can't guarantee one." He wiped the sweat off his forehead with his bare forearm. I tried hard to not recoil.

"Is that my only option?" I asked.

He shrugged. "You can wait here. Somebody will contact you when it's ready and you can either find a ride to Harperville or schedule somebody to deliver the car to you, but that might take a day or so."

Panic fluttered in my chest. My options sucked.

"I hope I'm not out of line, but I'm sure my aunt has a room available at the inn," Macey said. Her smile was radiant, and another flit that wasn't panic tickled my chest.

"There's an inn? What's it like?" Did I just rudely ask her that?

"It's a gorgeous old mansion that my aunt converted. I'm going to highly recommend it." She touched my arm again. "And there's Wi-Fi."

"I guess I'll just wait here for the dealership to call me." Who was I? I never took risks like this before. The driver stood my suitcase in front of me and nodded before leaving me stranded in a quirky place with bungalow homes, manicured lawns, a charming town square, and the nicest people. Things could've been worse. I could've been stuck in a small space with the tow truck driver. After glancing in the cab at the empty Red Bull cans and crumpled-up fast food bags that had piled up on the passenger seat and on the floor, I knew riding with him was my last option.

"You can store your things in the library. I can lock them up. You can work there or go on a tour with me if you're up for it," Macey said.

"You've been nothing but kind to me since I stalled here. I appreciate the offer, but I don't want to take you away from your job any more than I already have." I didn't mind going for a walk around the town square, but the heat was awful and I didn't want to melt in front of her. I also didn't want to miss the dealership's call.

"It's not a problem. It'll give me the opportunity to check in with some of my friends," she said. She checked her watch. "It'll be a while before they call you."

Spending time with Macey was exactly what I needed. Tamsyn would be proud of me for taking the initiative and meeting new people. "As long as you don't mind."

After a short walk to the library, Macey locked up my suitcase, messenger bag, and suit jacket. I rolled up my sleeves and strolled beside her.

"Why did you become a veterinarian?" she asked.

"I've loved animals my whole life. I grew up with dogs, cats, and guinea pigs. I'm the person who looks for the pets at parties." I hated that I was socially awkward. How do you tell somebody new that in your life, animals were better companions than people?

"I get it. Animals love unconditionally and people, well, people are trickier sometimes," she said.

"Oh, that sounds ominous. Bad breakup?" I asked. I don't know why I pushed the subject since we just met, but she shrugged and never stopped the flow of conversation.

"Not bad, for once. We just kind of drifted apart. My girlfriend wanted more than I could give her. My work in the community is the most important thing to me, and she didn't like when she wasn't my only priority."

Two things just happened. First, Macey came out to me whether she realized it or not. Also, I was very confused. I didn't want to belittle her career choice, but small-town librarian literally screamed free time. Maybe she was super passionate about her job, or maybe she was involved with the school and that took a lot of time, too. It wasn't my place to judge.

"I get that. My girlfriend broke up with me a little over a year ago for the same reasons. Late nights, on call a lot, and I work most weekends. I didn't miss a beat when she packed up and left." I wanted to ask if Ladybug Junction had a large LGBTQ+ community, but I already knew the answer.

Macey stopped below a sign that read Good Fortune and pushed open the glass door with a red frame. It was quaint and smelled like cinnamon and apples. The scent was sharp and my eyes watered at the incense smoke billowing from a tiny cone near the door. Macey pulled me further into the store.

"Good Fortune is very popular with visitors. It has everything from fresh flowers to greeting cards to candy and stuffed animals. Also, my friend Alyssa owns it."

We were greeted by an attractive woman who reminded me of one of our vet techs. Long red hair, pale skin, and a slender body. Alyssa didn't hide her frame beneath oversized clothing like our tech did. A bright yellow cold-shouldered shirt emphasized perky breasts and a small waist. The blue jeggings were slightly dated, but her confidence made me forget the fashion faux pas.

"Where have you been? I expected you earlier today," Alyssa said. She gave me an up and down, lifted an eyebrow at Macey, and bit back a grin. "Oh, never mind."

"Alyssa, this is Sawyer. Her car broke down just down the street, so she's waiting to hear back from the dealership in Harperville. Sawyer, this is my bestie, Alyssa."

"It's nice to meet you," I said. I looked around and nodded as though my approval made a difference. "What a cool place you have here." Honestly, it wasn't any different than a random gift shop you'd find in any strip mall, airport, or hospital, but I could see the pride on her face and knew I'd said the right thing.

"I'm so sorry about your car, but you're in excellent hands. Macey's the best," she said.

I gave them privacy to catch up and wandered the store picking up little knickknacks. Thankfully, Alyssa's store wasn't all about ladybugs. Some of the little crystal figurines were antiques, so I gave them a wide berth. Today wasn't my lucky day and I didn't want to take any chances breaking something else expensive. I glanced at my phone to see if I had any missed calls. My surprise at how quickly the time had passed was replaced by anxiety. What if they called and needed my approval? "Do you have Wi-Fi?" I asked as I pulled up available networks.

"Yes. Look for the GoodFortuneR40.2. The password is Alyssa10."

I nodded my thanks and excused myself as my phone buzzed silently, displaying a number I didn't recognize. "Hello, this is Sawyer Noel."

"Ms. Noel, this is Sunlight Chevrolet, and your Climateer was just delivered for repair. Unfortunately, the service department is closing up for the weekend, so we won't be able to get started on it until next week."

"Do you know what's wrong with it?"

The annoyance in his voice was unmistakable. "We won't know until we put it on the lift. I can't guarantee we'll even get to it on Monday. We'll have to get back to you next week."

I gritted my teeth to keep from spitting my anger out. "No, there's no getting back to me. I need a day and time when I can get my car. I'm without transportation in a town I've never been to. I'm going to need you to do better. I paid extra for service you're not giving me."

"Hold on." Soft harp music wafted in my ear while I waited. Bitter regret filled my mouth as I took a deep breath and released it. I was to blame for everything about my situation. A solid five minutes passed before my call was picked up.

"Ms. Noel, I just took a quick peek under your car. There's a sizable dent in the battery compartment, but I don't think there's a lot of damage. Unless we find something major, we can return your car Tuesday morning. Maybe Monday evening if everything checks out. We'll call you either way so if you're in a bind, we can get a loaner to you."

"Thank you. I'll expect your call Monday." I disconnected the call, proud of myself for making a quick decision. Now if I could only get rid of the unsettling feeling that burned in the pit of my stomach.

"Is everything okay?"

I looked into Macey's bright, shining hazel eyes. "Looks like I'm here until at least Monday. That noise we heard was me scraping and denting one of the batteries. They said it didn't look too bad, but they'd get back to me on Monday."

Her perfect smile made my regret less painful. "Well then, let's get you over to my aunt's."

❖

"I'm fine. The car's banged up. Really, I just needed to vent." I unzipped my suitcase, careful not to wrinkle my suits, and looked at my dismal selection of casual clothes. I dropped my phone on the bed after hitting the speaker icon to keep the call active. Tamsyn was a minute from dropping everything and racing to Ladybug Junction to save me.

"I'm sorry I romanticized a road trip. I thought it was a good idea to go for a leisurely drive and just think about opening up your own place. I didn't think you'd get stranded. I mean, it's a brand-new car." Thankfully, she didn't dwell on it. "But I can come get you and we can get a rental car."

The trip back home was four hours. Tamsyn didn't have the time for an eight-hour road trip. As much as I was teetering about her offer, I didn't want to impose. She was the busiest person I knew. "Thanks, but this will give me the opportunity to get out of my comfort zone. And I can polish up my speech."

Tamsyn snorted. "Is there a bar you can hang out at? Or is it a dry town?"

I frowned trying to recall if I had seen any neon signs or taverns around the square. "I don't know. Maybe Aunt Abby has a bar downstairs in the foyer."

"Who? Wait. You didn't hit your head, did you? Aunt Abby?"

"The lady who runs the inn."

"You're on a first-name basis? Maybe I really should come and get you."

I grabbed the phone off the bed and nestled it between my shoulder and ear. I didn't want anybody to hear Tamsyn in case the walls were thin. "No, it's Macey's aunt. I literally met her like five minutes ago."

"Who's Macey?"

I plopped down on the bed and sighed and told her the whole story and not just the I-banged-up-my-car part.

"Oh, so Macey just happens to be a hot, single lesbian librarian from a quaint town who is more than willing to drop everything and give you a tour? Come on. Really? No wonder you don't want me to pick you up. Stay. Practice your speech, eat greasy food, and maybe check out the local library," she said.

I could almost picture her giving me a coy wink and an elbow nudge if she was standing next to me.

"Keep me posted and be careful. Small towns are cute, but also we've seen enough horror movies to know better," she said.

I sent her a pin of my location after I disconnected the call. She wasn't wrong. I looked out the window but didn't see anything that gave me pause. The shadiest-looking person I ran into today was the tow truck driver, and he was an outsider. Everyone in town seemed normal. I hung up my jacket and made my way downstairs.

"Ms. Noel. We're so happy to have you. Will you be joining us for dinner at six?" Aunt Abby asked.

I checked my watch. It was just now five. I had an hour to kill. I wasn't hungry because of the late lunch, but I was a stress eater. "Yes, thank you." Also, I had nowhere else to be and no way to get there.

"Feel free to hang out in the lounge or sunroom. We have puzzles and games. Or take a walk around the gardens. We have several benches in the shade. The flowers are in full bloom." She pointed to a large pitcher of ice water with slices of lemon. "And help yourself to something cold to drink."

The sweet smell of roses, lilies, and hibiscus greeted me when I opened the back door. The garden was beautiful. I found a shaded bench and pulled up my speech, wanting to practice it, but my mind kept straying to Macey. Tamsyn was right. What were the odds I'd meet somebody like Macey in a place like this? The town was a blip on a map and somewhere I'd never think twice about stopping, but here I was renting a room for two days wondering if we had some kind of connection.

"Hey, you."

I looked up from my phone to find Macey a few feet away. It was as if she knew I was thinking about her. "Hi. What are you doing here?" My voice was a full octave higher than normal. It was obvious I was pleased to see her. I told myself to chill. I leaned back and pointed to the space beside me. "Have a seat."

"Thank you. My aunt invited me to dinner and I thought it would be nice to share another meal together." She tilted her head. "Are you feeling okay? You look flushed."

"It's fine. I'm sure I just got overheated today."

She pointed to my glass. "Drink up. Stay hydrated." She touched my arm. "I know you're stressed right now. Hopefully, you get your car back soon, but I like that you're here for a few days. I have a feeling you need some downtime and rest."

"I love my job, but this whole trip was a mistake," I said.

"Because your car broke down?"

"Not that specifically, but that certainly hasn't helped. My boss told me to take the whole week off instead of just a few days, but I hate to be away from my patients. I know that sounds silly since they are animals and most of them just need shots or a wellness exam, but I love them."

"And yet you don't have any pets. I find that interesting," Macey said.

I'd told her about losing my beagle right after Christina dumped me. I wasn't ready to replace him yet. It was going to take time.

She sat up. "Oh, you'll have to meet the love of my life, Ollie, since you'll be here a bit."

"That would be great." I meant it. Hedgehogs were popping up as popular pets, and it would be a good idea to get comfortable with them. We had our first sugar glider patient, and I was in love. The other veterinarians couldn't have cared less, but I was all about learning new animals and how to treat them. That's why they picked me for the conference. Well, that and the fact that Meredith and I were at each other's throats. I shook thoughts of her out of my head. She didn't deserve the space. "This is such a beautiful and quiet place." The stillness was punctuated by an occasional bird tweeting and some kind of alarm chirping off in the distance.

"They're working on the dam by the river." Macey twirled her hand to indicate the construction activity that was somewhere behind us. "But normally it's pretty quiet around here." She had changed her clothes and fixed her hair differently. Her wild curls were tamed back into a French braid and she was wearing a white sleeveless top and a khaki-colored skirt. Her brown sandals showed off a small tattoo on the top of her foot and a silver toe ring. I couldn't tell what the ink was and I didn't want to stare.

"What cool things happen in Ladybug Junction?"

"We do a lot of family stuff. As you know, most of my family lives here. And we have pop-up festivals every season."

"What's your favorite festival?" I fell in love with small-town life on the television show *Hart of Dixie*. There was always a fair or carnival, and everyone seemed so happy. I was getting the same vibe here.

"Definitely fall festival. I mean, who doesn't love pumpkin spice everything?" Macey's voice rose with her excitement level.

"I do have a soft spot for pumpkin baked goods."

"It's the first weekend in October and it's wonderful. We have pumpkin everything. Pumpkin spice lattes, pumpkin pies, pumpkin ale, pumpkin ravioli. I could go on and on."

I wasn't a massive pumpkin fan, but I wasn't going to rain on Macey's parade. "Our fall festival is all about the corn maze."

"When is your celebration?" she asked.

It was always the second weekend in October. I remembered because my ex-girlfriend and I fought because the festival landed on our anniversary weekend, but the clinic had a booth at the festival where we offered up pet adoptions and cheap shots for dogs and cats and I was picked to run it. "The week after yours."

"Sounds like you should come here for mine and I should go there for yours," she said. That sounded like a date to me.

I tried to disguise my surprise. "That would be great." Even though I wasn't sure ours would be as charming as hers. She was way too excited, and I was afraid she would be disappointed in how commercial ours was with cell phone provider booths, credit card booths, and how there was always at least one arrest for disorderly conduct. I didn't like to go every year because a lot of the same booths were there and it was too crowded.

"Ladies, dinner is ready." Aunt Abby peered out the kitchen window and waved to us in case her words didn't drift across the foliage. Macey nodded and stood.

"If you liked lunch, you're going to love dinner," she said.

I followed Macey to the charming dining area and sat with her at one of the four round tables.

"Do you need any help?" Macey raised her voice so her aunt could hear.

"Oh, no. You keep our guest company and I'll be back with two plates."

Macey shrugged. "She never lets me help. Ever."

"Are you a good cook?" I asked.

"Not really. I can serve food, take her world-famous biscuits out of the oven, and make a few things." She looked around the empty dining room in surprise. "It's just us."

I poured a glass of lemon water from the jug on the table. "So, you're nice, hospitable, like to canoe, but you can't cook. I found your one weakness."

She playfully threw her arms up. "Everyone in my family works in the food industry. One would think I would've learned, but instead they just shooed me out of the kitchen."

"And you had nothing to do but read. Am I right?" I asked. She laughed. I liked hearing Macey's laugh. It felt genuine and made my stomach flutter. She was utterly charming. Just like everything about Ladybug Junction.

"You're right. Maybe it was my destiny."

I didn't realize how close I was leaning into the conversation until Aunt Abby tried to serve us dinner. We both leaned back.

"Chicken and waffles made with my own secret recipe," she said.

I looked at my full plate and knew I was going to eat most of it. What was wrong with me? I never ate like this. I was a salad girl who occasionally ate salmon or grilled steak. I avoided carbs and sweets, yet here I was eating pie and waffles on the same day. Was I trying to impress Macey, or did I just not give a fuck because I was on a mini vacation?

"This looks and smells delicious. Thank you so much." I wasn't paying enough to stay here to receive this kind of attention. I was definitely going to give them a five-star review on Google and Yelp. I already knew my headline: *Quaint and Perfect.* We took over two hours to finish our meal. I was sad when Macey said she had to go but that she would be back in the morning. She had the day off and promised to show me around and introduce me to her Oliver.

"Get some sleep and I'll see you in the morning." I leaned against one of the columns of the entrance to the bed-and-breakfast and watched Macey walk up the street and turn out of sight. What a strange twenty-four hours. Even though I was essentially stranded here, I felt safe. The anxiety I fought daily was gone. Maybe it was Macey or maybe it was small-town life, but whatever it was, I was at peace, and that was a feeling I hadn't had in years.

Chapter Three

He is the cutest thing I've ever seen. Also, very squirmy." I held Ollie in my hands and watched as he sniffed and tried to escape. Not in a panicky way, but in a way that said he had better things to do with his time. His quills poked my palms and I struggled to keep him in my grasp.

"It takes time for hedgehogs to bond with their handlers. We've been at it for two years now," she said. She picked up Ollie and flipped him so he was on his back. His quills relaxed when she rubbed his pink tummy. I leaned closer to get a better look, not realizing that I was completely in her personal space. The energy between us shifted. She turned her head to smile at me, and when her gaze dropped down to my lips, I gently leaned back. Fear won over bravery. In my head, I was smooth and brushed my lips across hers, but in reality, I was too nervous. And I was horrible with vibes, especially around women. Tamsyn joked that I was broken, and even though we laughed about it, a part of my heart felt no truer words had been spoken.

"He seems sweet. Are they all good-natured or is he an exception?" I asked. I carefully touched his belly and smiled at the soft warmth until the moment he screamed at me. I quickly pulled my hand back and created space. "I'm so sorry."

"Don't worry about it. He's not really a people hedgehog," she said.

"Has he ever been to a vet?" I asked.

She placed him gently in the cutest five-by-five-foot area fenced off with a ten-inch high, white picket fence. "Nope. He's a healthy little boy. I know this looks extreme, but he really has a good time in his tiny town." She had plastic tunnels for him to race through, tiny soccer balls for him to play with, a doll pool with an inch of water, and other toys. There were small houses that he could crawl into and nap.

I couldn't stop smiling. "I think it's impressive."

"Most people don't understand my love for him. They wouldn't get this setup. Thank you for loving animals as much as I do," she said.

"You should see our office. We have two cats, Sheldon and Syd, who have several beds and kitty condos around. We're constantly picking up after them, so I totally get this." I swirled my finger indicating all of Ollie's Way, the name that hung from a tiny sign on the fence. At least it wasn't obnoxiously perfect. It was just cute. After a solid hour of playing with him, Macey thought giving him alone time would be good.

"Let's let him play or nap or whatever he wants to do. He's not used to this much stimulation," Macey said.

"Is he good to be out like this?"

"Totally. He loves alone time. We'll check in on him later," she said.

I felt chills when her fingers touched mine as she helped me up from my sitting position. She kept a grasp on my hand for a few moments until I stood in front of her. "Today has been such a great day."

We had spent the last six hours together getting to know one another. We hiked, biked, ate butter pecan cones from the ice cream parlor on the town square, and talked nonstop. It was a steady flow of questions and answers, funny stories, and soft, flirty touches. I was positive she was interested in me, but I was too much of a chicken shit to make a move. She seemed too good to be true. Plus, what kind of relationship could we have? She lived four hours from me, and the trip wasn't exactly easy.

"What's on your mind?" she asked.

I frowned. "What do you mean?"

"You seemed to have just slipped away from the moment. Is everything okay?"

Just me self-sabotaging a relationship that I wasn't sure really existed. "I'm fine. I'm just thinking about the conference."

"If you're worried about being in front of a crowd, you can always practice your speech on me," she said.

I waved her off. "Oh, no. I wouldn't want anyone to voluntarily subject themselves to a boring speech about pets and obesity." I blushed. Nobody had ever offered to listen to any of my speeches before. And that wasn't what was on my mind anyway. "Speaking of which, I should probably get back to my room and get geared up for it." I smiled when Macey's face fell.

"And we were having such a fun time, but I get it. How about I come over later for a glass of wine tonight and we sit out in the garden for a bit?"

Like I was going to say no. "That sounds great." I checked my watch. "How about eight?" I knew she didn't work tomorrow, but I didn't know when the dealership would call with news on my car. They might call first thing and I didn't want to miss out on the opportunity to have a few more minutes with her.

"Perfect. I'll see you there. You know how to get back to the inn, right?" We had moved closer to the front door and were lingering in the foyer.

I thumbed behind me. "Just three blocks that way and a quick right."

"Okay. I'll see you later," she said.

I slipped outside into the stifling evening. It was amazing that even though the humidity and heat weighed me down the moment I stepped outside, my heart felt light and airy. I slid my hands in my pockets and strolled back to the inn. I had a few text messages from Tamsyn and a missed call from my mother. I messaged Tamsyn that I was good and would call her after I got news about the car, but I called my mom.

"How's the conference?" she asked.

Did I tell her the truth and have her worry about me? "I'll be there on Tuesday night. I still have a few days."

"Don't overdo it. I know how hard you like to work," she said.

"Only when I'm dealing with animals and not people." She knew I wasn't overly fond of public speaking, but knew I was passionate about my topic. "What did you do this weekend?"

I was deflecting. The last thing I wanted to do was give my mom any ammunition or false hope just because I was talking to a woman. I spent ten minutes getting caught up with her knowing that if I didn't have this conversation now, she would hound me every day during the conference. After I disconnected the call and met all stay-in-touch obligations, I pulled out my laptop and practiced my speech until the room phone rang, startling me back to reality.

"Hi, Sawyer. I'm downstairs with the most fabulous bottle of Pinot. Are you still up for a glass?" That light, airy feeling returned to my chest. I slammed my laptop shut and checked my appearance in the mirror. I was embarrassed that I didn't have anything to wear except suits and workout clothes, so I was wearing a pair of leggings and a Nike T-shirt. I sighed and made my way to the sitting room. Macey's hair was damp from a recent shower and I could smell her lavender soap. I felt like a swamp rat next to her and regretted not showering.

"Hi," I said.

"Hello." She quirked her head to the side and smiled.

Although her eyes never left mine, I could feel her checking me out. "So, tell me about this wine," I said.

She motioned her head over to the small bar nestled next to the stocked bookshelf and pulled out two glasses. "It's not from Ladybug Junction, if that's what you're thinking. It's a Pinot Grigio that Alyssa picked up when she was in Italy. I've been saving it for a special occasion and decided tonight was special enough."

I raised my eyebrows and nodded. "I'm excited to try something new." I didn't focus on the fact that I was her special occasion. I took the glass from her hand and sat with my back against the armrest of the couch so I could face her comfortably. She did the same. Time flew when I was with Macey. We sat on the couch until midnight. I had to stop and think about what day it was and how long I had before the conference. My speech was on Thursday morning. There was a cocktail meet and greet Tuesday night before the convention officially got underway Wednesday morning.

"You're doing that thing again where you disappear," Macey said.

I tilted my head to process her words and smiled sheepishly. "You caught me. I was trying to figure out my schedule this week and when I need to be in Atlanta."

"Your speech is Thursday, right? What other panels or speeches interest you?" she asked.

I knew nobody was that interested in my life. "I'll probably attend everything. It never hurts to learn as much as you can, especially if I'm seriously considering opening my own business," I said. Macey was the only other person I told besides Tamsyn. The more people who knew, the more it became a possibility.

"I think it's great when people want to be their own boss. And with your heart for animals, I can't imagine you won't do well. Little Ollie loved you and he just met you," she said.

"Let's be real. He tolerated me until I touched him. Then he screamed."

Macey laughed. "Yes, but he trusted you enough and that speaks volumes." She looked at her watch. "It's so late. I should go. Did Aunt Abby even say good night to us?"

I nodded. "She poked her head in about an hour ago and waved, but you were busy pouring us another glass." I had drunk more wine in the last two days than I had in the last two months. I was a brandy drinker with an occasional beer at dinner. Alcohol wasn't my thing. I was on call too much. I followed her into the kitchen to rinse my glass and recycle the bottle. "Thanks for keeping me company the last two days. If it wasn't for you, I'd probably be stuck in a sterile hotel room in Harperville for days. You've made hanging around and waiting fun."

"If you need a ride to the dealership, I will totally take you. I'm off tomorrow."

"Are you trying to get rid of me?" I asked.

She slid closer to me and touched my hand. "Absolutely not. This has been the most fun I've had in a long time." Her voice dropped to almost a whisper and her fingers interlocked with mine. There was no mistaking that she was interested.

I had to make my move or regret this decision for a very long time. I cupped her chin with my hand. "Thank you for saving me," I said. I slowly brushed my lips across hers. When she didn't move, I pressed harder and ran my tongue on her bottom lip before capturing it in my mouth. I felt that kiss from the tips of my toes to the flush across my cheeks. She was warm and slid closer to my body until her arms were around my waist. I held her close and deepened the kiss. My tongue touched hers, softly at first, until we fell into the perfect rhythm. It became obvious that we were either going to have to stop or take it upstairs to the privacy of my room.

She pulled back first. "Wow." She put her fingers up to her lips as though trying to keep the kiss there longer. Her reaction was exactly what my confidence needed.

"That was really nice," I said. What did one say after such a kiss? I knew there would be a strong reaction if we crossed the line, but I didn't know that we would sizzle like this.

"I should go home. It's getting late," she said.

Everything about her body language said she didn't want to go. I didn't have the desire to make out in her aunt's inn. Maybe if we were at her house, tonight would have a different ending. "I can walk you home," I said.

"Then I would have to walk you home and we'd do this back and forth all night until morning." Her hazel eyes were dark and her voice shaky. She cleared her throat and took another step back.

"And I think I'm going to go ahead and leave tomorrow," I said.

"Oh? Did you finally hear back from the dealership?"

I could almost see her shutting down. I sighed knowing I was the reason this special moment ended. "No, but either way, I have to get on the road tomorrow. I'm starting to panic about getting there." It meant leaving Ladybug Junction early, but I had a plan. "I'm thinking about stopping back by on my way home." Her genuine pearly white smile told me my idea had merit. "I mean, if that's okay."

Her lips met mine and I couldn't tell which one of us moaned. Maybe we both did. She felt soft and supple in my arms and we were back in the predicament of either stopping or going to my room.

This time, I pulled away. "How about dinner Saturday night? A real date. We can hit the cute Italian restaurant on the corner if you'd like." It was the only other restaurant I noticed in town.

"I have a better idea. Why don't I cook dinner for us instead?" she asked. Just yesterday she said she was a horrible cook, but I wasn't stupid enough to challenge her. She wanted alone time with me, and I was all for it.

"I think that sounds wonderful," I said.

She kissed me hard this time. It felt like I went from zero to sixty in a second. Her fingertips slipped under my T-shirt and chills sped along my skin right behind her touch. "Okay. I'm going to stop and bottle this for next weekend." She scraped her front teeth along her bottom lip and held the pose. She was so damn sexy.

"I've never been more excited for the weekend," I said. A burst of energy circled inside me, gaining momentum with every heartbeat, and even though it was after midnight, I knew I wouldn't get a lot of sleep. I had a date with an incredible woman who didn't have any baggage and was available. She was four hours away, but I was willing to see where this would go. "Good night, Macey."

"Good night, Sawyer."

❖

The start to the conference was a blur. I met a ton of new people who inspired me and encouraged me to start my own business. I had a list of panels I wanted to attend every day, and I spent every meal reconnecting and networking with colleagues. Even so, the most exciting part was checking my phone and seeing text messages from Macey.

Is your car still good?

If anyone was watching me, they would have thought I just won the lottery. When I smiled this big, I knew I looked like a giant cheeseball. *I haven't driven it since I parked it. And I will charge it in Harperville before Saturday so I'll make it from LJ to my house.*

Sounds like an excellent plan. Can't wait to see you again.

I tried to pretend that it didn't mean anything. That her excitement wasn't affecting me. Was Macey the real deal? I hadn't felt this lightheaded about another woman in forever. Tamsyn was going to love her. *I can't wait either. Okay. I have to pay attention.*

Am I distracting you? She ended her text with a smiley face emoji wearing a halo.

In the best possible way. Talk to you tonight. I'd spent the last two nights talking to Macey on the phone for hours. Last night we talked about our dreams. She gave me sound, encouraging advice about starting my own business. Financially, I could do it, but mentally it was going to take its toll. Long hours with very little downtime. That would curb my social life a lot, and I barely had one as it was. Plus, that meant if things continued with Macey, finding alone time would be hard.

I brushed thoughts of Macey and a possible relationship

from my brain so I could concentrate on the discussion about parasites and pets. My presentation was immediately after this one. I had reviewed my speech so much that I almost knew it by heart. When it was my turn at the podium, I quickly hooked up my laptop, got a crash course from a techie on how to move my slides with a clicker they swiftly plugged into my computer, and stared at the time. I saw a lot of familiar faces in the crowd, and even though I was pleased with the turnout, standing room only was daunting.

"Hello. Thank you for coming. I'm Dr. Sawyer Noel from Oliver Strong Clinic in Shreveport, Louisiana. Today we're going to talk about obesity and the dangers of having an overweight pet." I slipped into my speech and answered several questions at the end. I felt it was a successful presentation because the attendees still with questions followed me out into the hall so we could make room for the next session. By the time I got back to my room, I was both exhausted and pumped up. I was supposed to grab drinks with new people in our field, including an attractive vet technician who seemed interested in more than just our chat. If I wasn't so damn excited about Macey, I would have flirted back. I went from a bad breakup over a year ago to two beautiful, smart women who were into me. Maybe my dry spell was over.

CHAPTER FOUR

A nd you said you couldn't cook." I inhaled deeply when I walked into Macey's house. Garlic and a variety of spices wafted in the air.

She walked ahead of me carrying the small bouquet of flowers I picked up in Harperville on my way back to Ladybug Junction. "Don't be fooled. Anyone can make spaghetti and garlic bread. Also, thank you for the flowers. They're beautiful." She quickly added them to a crystal vase and placed them on the table.

"All of this looks incredible. I skipped lunch to save room for dinner." I left the conference right after breakfast, skipping the afternoon closing reception. I didn't want to be there. I wanted to be here, with Macey, and act on these blossoming feelings.

"It's about the only thing I know how to cook," she said. She stirred the sauce and added noodles to the boiling water. "Dinner should be ready in about ten minutes. Can I pour you a glass of wine?" A thin golden chain dangled from her neck as she leaned over the table to pour two glasses of Cabernet Sauvignon. She handed me one.

"Thank you," I said.

"You look great," she said. She smiled and raised an eyebrow. "Really great."

I felt warmth swirl inside and push against my skin. I spent a lunch hour shopping at the mall across the street from the conference center and picked up a few casual but nice outfits knowing I was going to spend the weekend in Ladybug Junction. I wanted to look fresh and chill, not professional and uptight like the last time I was here. Tonight, I was wearing high waist ankle pants and a deep V-neck button-up fitted shirt. "Thank you. You look amazing."

She looked beautiful. I wanted to touch the adorable curls that escaped the bun and framed her heart-shaped face and high cheekbones. And run my fingers down her slender neck. She wore a red summer dress that showed a generous amount of smooth skin. It was hard not to stare at the soft vertical line that peeked out from the sweetheart neckline. Macey was a dream come true. She ticked all my boxes that I looked for in a woman. She was friendly, attractive, genuine, and gave me one hundred percent of her attention. It was early, but I had yet to find something wrong with her. In my head, I heard Tamsyn telling me to get out of my comfort zone and go for it.

"Are you closer to making a decision about opening your own practice? Were you able to get in touch with that one colleague from college?" she asked.

Macey was a great listener and liked to talk on the phone. Thursday night, we talked until almost one in the morning. I was so pumped from my presentation that I called her and we slipped into one of the best conversations I'd had in a long time.

"I did. She gave me sound advice, but also didn't sugarcoat it. She said it was hard work and told me to find an existing place that I could convert into a clinic. Then when I become established, I can build my dream practice from the ground up." I jumped in to help carry food to the table. "It makes perfect sense."

"You probably have a lot of clients who will follow you if you strike out on your own. You said you were always given extreme cases, and let me tell you, people remember when you go above and beyond. I bet once they find out, they'll switch to you." She sounded so convincing.

"I'm going to need daily affirmations from you if I do it," I said.

She smiled and nodded. "I can do that."

Even though everything smelled delicious, I fixed a light plate. Too many carbs would put me in a coma, and I wanted to be alert. I was excited. This was my first real date in forever.

"I know this is probably too much." Macey waved her arms over the table. "But I come from a long line of foodies, and this is how we show we care."

"It looks amazing. I just don't want to fall asleep on you tonight."

"I promise you won't."

I felt a little jolt at the way her lips curved into a smile that hinted at something a little more than just friendship. Again, I blushed. I was horrible at flirting. I stood there like a block of wood. She pointed to the chair opposite her. "Have a seat."

"So, you know all about my big dream in life. What are yours? No, wait. Let me guess. You have the voice of an angel and you're planning on winning one of those reality singing competitions."

She almost snorted. "Oh, my God, no. I have a horrible singing voice. And no, you will never hear it. I'm that bad."

"Come on. You have the sweetest talking voice. I can't imagine your singing one is bad."

"Really. It's not even singing. It's more like croaking. My mom is the singer in our family. And even my uncle has a nice voice. So, no. Singing isn't my dream," she said.

"Okay, so not singing. How about FBI agent? People wouldn't think such a charming woman could be so sneaky." I took a bite and waited for her to argue that logic, too.

"Would you believe published writer?" she asked.

I could tell she was serious, so I cast all joking aside. "Definitely. Librarians are smart and ambitious. Do you have anything in the works?"

"I have a rough draft, but nothing ready to submit anywhere."

Her self-confidence faltered a little. I reached out and gave her hand a squeeze.

"I'm sure it's great." I leaned back and relaxed my shoulders. "Tell me about it." She shrugged.

"Are you a reader?" she asked.

"I read a lot of nonfiction." I cringed knowing that wasn't what she wanted to hear. She looked slightly disappointed. "If I had more time, I'd read fiction, but I'm still learning so much about my field." I had to dig deep to remember the last fiction book I read. I snapped my fingers when the title of the book slipped into my mind. "*Where the Crawdads Sing*. That was the last book I read."

"Good choice. My book is nothing like that. It's more of a young adult dystopian," she said. Her eyes lit up as she launched into the plot. I couldn't help but be excited with her. She gestured wildly with her arms, explaining how the world ends and what people have to do in order to survive.

"I can picture everything you described. It would make a great movie," I said.

"I wish! But baby steps. I need to read through it and then figure out if I'm going to submit it anywhere or self-publish. And I need to find an editor to polish it."

"Tough decision, but also congrats on finishing a book. That's not an easy thing."

"Thank you. I'm pretty proud of it. How exciting would it be to sign with a publishing company out of New York City? I'm sure that doesn't happen except for in the movies, but it's always nice to dream."

"A dreamer like me. It's a good thing we found each other," I said.

Macey tipped her glass against mine. "I'll drink to that."

I liked the way her hazel eyes glowed in the candlelight. "How about we sit out on the porch for a bit? It's a nice night." I helped her clear the table before we turned off the porch light and sat very close together on the porch swing. She slid her hand into mine as we chatted about the azalea flowers that blossomed in front of the house. I pretended that it wasn't a big deal that my heart felt like it was skipping in place or how my skin tingled against hers. I couldn't help but stare at her.

Her eyes twinkled in the moonlight as she stared up at the stars. "You probably don't see stars this bright in the big city."

"You're right. This is beautiful. Small-town life has its charms for sure." I took a deep breath and blew it out slowly. The town was quiet only because I didn't hear the beat of traffic or the scurrying of people as they moved about their lives. Once I figured out how to relax, new sounds presented themselves. The high, continuous chirp of cicadas and the low, constant croaks of bullfrogs filled the night air and gave me a sense of peace. I turned to Macey. "When was the last time you visited Shreveport?"

She leaned her head on her palm as she rested her elbow on the back of the bench. "It's been a long time, but I'd like to see it again."

I liked the way she looked at me. Her eyes drifted down to my mouth. After the third time of her dreamy gaze, I leaned forward and pressed my lips against hers. It felt right. She scooted closer into my arms and put her hand on my thigh. My body flamed instantly. I cupped her face and kissed the corners of her mouth, her cheek, and placed a trail of kisses along the curve of her neck. Her pulse quickened under my lips, and the passion from last weekend rushed back into focus. It was hard to break apart, but we were out in the open for all of Ladybug Junction to see.

"Maybe we should go inside," I said. I felt her nod and squeeze my thigh tighter. We stood at the same time. Our bodies brushed and it was so hard not to press myself against her.

"Good idea." She held my fingers tightly and pulled me into her house. The moment the door latched shut, my back was pressed up against it and she was in my arms. "I'm so glad you're here."

I didn't get a chance to answer. Her mouth was on mine. The

velvet tip of her tongue ran across my lips until I parted them. She tasted like wine and smelled like the honeysuckle bushes outside the window. My knees threatened to buckle when I felt her warm hands slip under my shirt and run across my stomach.

"Let's go back to my room."

I stopped her hands and linked my fingers with hers. "Are you sure? This isn't too fast?" I held my breath as I waited for her answer. We had no idea what the future was going to be like, but we had right now, and I didn't want her to have any regrets.

"I've been thinking about this all week," she said.

Her fingers quickly unbuttoned my shirt as she guided me back to her bedroom. A spark ignited in my stomach and burned along the path her fingertips traveled across my skin. I shrugged the shirt off my shoulders and pulled her close for a deep kiss. I sucked her bottom lip into my mouth and ran my tongue across its fullness before slipping my tongue inside. She moaned and fell against me trying to rid herself of her dress. I turned her around and quickly unzipped her dress with incredible finesse as though I had been doing it forever. Her bare back was sexy and smooth and I pressed my body against hers, feeling her warmth against my breasts. I kissed the back of her neck and linked my fingers with hers. Another delicious moan ripped from her lips when I raised her arms above her head and pushed my hips into her. I was never this bold, but with Macey I felt like a different person. She made me feel alive.

"You're incredible." I sounded breathy. When I released her hands to pull her hips into mine, she left her palms flat against the wall. Her passion elevated my pulse and made me lightheaded. "How close is your room?" We were somewhere in the hall, and I couldn't remember if her bedroom was down the hall or one of the closer doors.

"Last door on the left," she said.

Her dress had fallen to gather at her waist, exposing her breasts. I was torn between dropping to my knees here in the hallway, stripping her dress completely off, losing myself between her legs, or guiding her back to her bedroom where I could take my time learning every curve, soft spot, and where she liked to be touched. Seeing her breasts heave while she gasped for breath answered for me. I needed to feel her body in my arms and her body pressed against mine. I wanted to slowly kiss every part of her and watch her move against me. I grabbed her hand and pulled her into her room until the back of my thighs hit the mattress.

"You're so beautiful," I said. I cupped her full breasts and ran my thumbs across her hard nipples. I watched her pupils grow in the soft light from the nightstand lamp. "Let your hair down."

She obliged. Corkscrew curls framed her face and cascaded down her shoulders. She was breathtaking. I pulled down her dress and helped her step out of it. I smiled when I noticed the tattoo on her foot was a butterfly and, thankfully, not a ladybug. Her silk panties quickly followed.

"You're still dressed," she said.

I quickly kicked off my pants and crawled on top of her. I was on my hands and knees leaning over her. I kissed her while she unhooked my bra and let it slide down my arms. I brushed it off. The only thing left was my panties, but I was too anxious and needed to feel her body against mine. I sank into her. The panties would have to come off later. "Better?" I asked.

She slid her arms over my back and moved under me until I was cradled between her legs. "Now it's better," she said.

She was so wet and warm. She grabbed my ass and squeezed me closer to her. I slowly moved my hips and we both moaned. I couldn't remember the last time I felt this good. It had been over a year, and I kissed her mouth and scraped my teeth down her neck. She wrapped her hands in my hair and pushed me lower. I smiled at her enthusiasm. I was not a take-charge kind of lover, but I couldn't get enough of Macey and I would do anything to please her. I ran my tongue over her breasts sucking and nipping at the soft, sensitive skin. I held her hips and licked a path straight to her pussy. I spread her open and flattened my tongue against her throbbing clit. She bucked against me in pleasure and hissed out a breathy moan.

"That feels…" Macey's body grew taut after a hard lick. I slowed down and waited for her to find her voice. "That feels so good." My blood pounded in my head as instinct took over. I slipped one finger inside as I continued to softly lick her clit. She lifted her hips, wanting more. I added a second finger and pressed my tongue harder along her slit. This was going quicker than I imagined, but we had all night. I moved my fingers faster until her entire body tensed and an orgasm rippled through her. She barely made a sound. I wrapped her in my arms and held her close. I didn't care that we didn't make it under the sheets or that we were both covered in sweat.

"I'm sorry that was so fast, but—" I started.

She leaned up and put her finger on my lip. "Don't apologize." She kissed me swiftly. "We have all night."

"That's what I was just thinking."

"Oh? Looks like great minds think alike," she said.

I was going to ask what she had in mind, but her fluttering fingers across my body answered me. I closed my eyes and enjoyed her wandering hands and warm mouth as she got to know me. For the first time in a long time, I wasn't nervous about being naked around another person. Even though I'd only known Macey for a week, it felt longer. I trusted her. When her fingers trailed a path between my legs, I unabashedly spread them further apart. She kissed me when she entered me, and had her body not been holding mine down, I would have floated away. Sex with Macey was nice. I wanted to hold off on my orgasm because I hadn't had one that wasn't self-induced in over a year and I was selfish. I wanted it to last forever so I gritted my teeth and rewarded myself with a few extra seconds of hanging in the sweet spot of oblivion before I came. The rush of blood and pleasure flooded my body.

"Now I'm the one who's sorry," I said.

She looked at me. "Why are you sorry?"

"It's been a while. I'm a little rusty." I was always in it for the chase, and even though the sex was nice, I expected more fireworks.

"Hey, where'd you go?" she asked.

I'd realized my mind was wandering in weird directions and I needed to be in the moment. "Sorry. I'm probably more tired than I thought."

She sat up and pulled the comforter over us. I didn't sleep in the nude, but asking for clothes meant I'd have to take them off in a few hours.

"How's this?" she asked and rested her head on my shoulder and placed her arm over my stomach. Such a simple gesture brought a level of intimacy to my life that I didn't realize I missed until this moment.

"Perfect." The last thing I remember was pulling her closer to me and smiling as her warm body heated mine and her long curls tickled my skin.

❖

"Time to wake up," Macey said. I cracked one eye open and squinted at the bright light that spilled through the open curtains. She stood by the side of the bed.

"How do you have this much energy? I can barely function," I said, or maybe I thought it. I was so tired. I closed my eyes again.

"Wake up, Sawyer." I felt groggy and opened my eyes again. Macey was looking at me intently. I mumbled something and closed my eyes. The room was bright and I wondered how long I'd been asleep. "What time is it?"

"It's time."

"Can't we just stay like this for a little bit longer?" I glanced at the clock. It was nine and I was barely awake. The plan was to have a late lunch at Tilly's and then hit the road.

"Okay. But just for a few minutes," she said.

I must've fallen asleep because the next thing I remembered was her rocking my shoulder gently and staring at my face again. I smiled. "Hi again."

"Hi."

I tried to rub my eyes, but my arms felt heavy. "How long was I out for? I don't want to sleep the day away."

She looked deep into my eyes. "Too long. It's time."

I dropped my head back on the pillow and exhaled. "I don't want to leave."

"I know you don't, but so many people are waiting for you."

"I know." I closed my eyes again. Reality was creeping into my cocoon. "I know." I drifted off again.

Chapter Five

My throat was on fire and my body ached. Breathing even hurt. I tried opening my eyes, but they weren't cooperating. Everything was fuzzy from my tongue to my memories. I tried harder and managed to squint until I could see a little bit of my surroundings. The flowers were there but Macey's room felt different. It was brighter and colder than before. "Why is the alarm going off?" My lips stuck together so my question never made it out of my mouth. I tried swallowing, but my jaw was sore.

"Hi, sweetie. It sure is good to see you awake. Let me ring for the doctor," said a woman's voice I didn't recognize.

The voice wasn't Macey's, and that put me in full panic mode. The alarm got louder, faster, and my eyes widened in fear. Where the fuck was I? I felt a warm hand on my shoulder.

"I'm going to need you to relax. I'm Becky, your morning nurse. You're at Memorial Junction hospital in Shreveport. You were in a car accident," she said.

Car accident? How did I get to Shreveport? I heard her call somebody on the intercom in my room. I squeezed my eyes shut and tried to process her words and my life and how the two could possibly be intertwined. I was completely overwhelmed. I didn't remember being in an accident. I didn't remember going to the hospital. What the fuck happened?

"Dr. Burr will be here soon."

I nodded but didn't open my eyes. I felt her dab a tissue on my cheeks and my neck as several tears fell. It was the last thing I remembered before I faded out again. I didn't know if I'd fallen asleep for a few minutes or days. Every part of my body felt heavy. I turned my head when I heard the click of the door and felt a warm hand in mine.

"Try to stay awake, Sawyer. Can you focus on me? I'm Dr. Macey Burr, head of the neurology department at Memorial Junction Hospital. You were in a car accident and got a little banged up. Do you mind if I take a look at you?"

It was her, my dream girl, but she was different. I shook my head to try to rid my brain of the spiderwebs and fill in the missing gaps, but nothing fell into place.

"No? You don't want me to?" She leaned over me with her penlight ready to check my pupils.

I nodded slowly. I wasn't mad at her. I was mad at my brain. I needed answers.

"Good response in both your eyes. That's great. Do you know your full name?"

I nodded again, and even though in my head I was articulate and confident, it came out as a raspy whisper. "Sawyer." I paused and tried to clear my throat. "Noel."

She checked my pulse and listened to my heart. "Sawyer Noel. It's nice to meet you. Do you know what year it is?"

"Twenty-four." I didn't know the date and hoped I got the year right. Was I dreaming?

"Excellent," she said. She turned to the nurse. "Let's schedule a few tests and reach out to physical therapy to evaluate now that she's alert." She pulled out a small tool with a spiked roller at the end. It reminded me of something my grandmother had in her sewing basket. I had questions, but asking them wasn't easy, so I gave up.

"I'm going to just do a quick check. You've been in a medically induced coma for eight days, so your muscles are weak." She zipped the tool down both legs. I jumped and hissed out in pain when she ran it over my feet. "You're ticklish. I'm sorry, but I'm thrilled at your response. Let's try your right arm." I felt the spikes down each finger and all the way up my shoulder. "Your left arm is going to be trickier since it's in a cast."

It was the first time I noticed I couldn't straighten my arm and realized that the heaviness I felt across my chest was the clunky cast. I wiggled my fingers and a wave of relief washed over me when everything seemed to be working except for being able to bend my arm. I looked at Macey for an explanation.

"You fractured your elbow and they had to surgically repair it. You'll be in a fiberglass cast for at least six weeks and some physical therapy after that. Are you in any pain?"

Nothing felt normal. At my nod, she issued pain meds and asked the nurse to up my fluid intake. I focused on her mouth, and when she started talking about my family who were anxious to see me, my eyelids fluttered shut against my will. I was surrounded by darkness again.

❖

"Holy shit, you're awake."

Tamsyn leaned over me and started crying when I finally made eye contact with her. I tried to smile but my head hurt. "Stop," I said. Once one of us started crying, the other one did, too, and my head was already pounding. I didn't need stuffy sinuses on top of the pressure already built up behind my eyes.

"Yeah, I know the rule, but fuck, you scared me. You scared all of us." She grabbed my hand and squeezed my fingers. "I shouldn't have talked you into driving. If it wasn't for me, we'd be at Manny's eating tacos and drinking margaritas instead of here in a hospital praying that you're okay." She paused and gave a half sob before continuing. "You're okay, right?"

I nodded. "I don't remember anything." That was the longest sentence I'd said, and my head pounded with anger and the loudness of my words. I closed my eyes again.

"You don't remember anything? What does that mean? You have amnesia? Wait. Do you even know who I am?"

I wanted to smile at how theatrical she sounded, but her voice was so loud that I winced instead. I tried to shush her with a puff of breath and an awkward motion of trying to put my finger up to my lips but failed. "I couldn't forget you." I paused to catch my breath. "I don't remember the wreck." Why did my lungs hurt so badly?

"Wonderful. You're awake again." Macey walked into my line of vision and pulled up something on the computer in my room. "How are you feeling?"

"Like I got beat up. Everything hurts." I had no idea what was reality and what was fiction, and it scared the shit out of me. In my mind, I just left this woman's bed and yet she showed no other emotion than how a doctor would treat a patient.

"I believe that." She looked at Tamsyn. "I'm going to do a quick exam."

Tamsyn shot up before Macey could ask her to leave. "I'll call Lauren and tell her you're awake. I'll be back later. I'll send your mom and dad up. I think they're in the cafeteria. Shit, I'm rambling. Okay, I'm so happy, Sawyer." She squeezed my hand and left the room.

Macey poured a small cup of water and placed it on the tray by my bed. "Sounds like you might need this, but let's take it slow." She raised the bed so I was in a sitting position and held the glass with the straw pointed at me.

I leaned forward and took a small sip. It felt wonderfully cool against my raw throat. I took a second sip before she pulled the cup away.

"What's wrong with my throat?" I touched my neck and felt leads and electrodes all over my body. My hand was heavy and I dropped it in my lap. "What's wrong with everything?"

She touched my hand. "You hit your head when you rolled your car. We had to put you in a medically induced coma to allow the swelling in your brain to subside," she said. I must've had a horrified look on my face because she gave me a soft smile and touched my hand again. "It's a normal procedure when there's been any kind of head trauma. You were on a ventilator, so that's why your throat and sinuses hurt. The good news is that your MRI came back unremarkable." That was a word I wasn't expecting, but judging from her expression, that was a good thing. "You have two lacerations with sutures. One along your hairline and one on your left side on your rib cage." She gingerly touched the bandage on my head to inspect it.

I couldn't help but stare at her. I was confused by everything. I had tons of questions and didn't know how to ask them. "This is real life, right? This isn't a dream."

Her light laugh tugged at my heart. It was unfamiliar, but I felt it with every part of my body. "This is real," she said.

I sighed. That's exactly what somebody in a dream world would say.

"Starting tomorrow, you'll start physical therapy, and there are going to be several doctors who are going to check in on you to make sure everything is fine. We'll start you off with a liquid diet for a few days. Are you hungry?"

I was exhausted and tired and just wanted to sleep.

"Sawyer!"

My mom rushed past Macey to kiss my cheek. She held my face in her hands. "Oh, honey. I'm so happy you're awake. Tamsyn just told us."

I didn't tell her my head throbbed from the way she lifted it up from the pillow.

"Hi, Mom." Of course she started crying, and that made me tear up. "I'm fine." I wasn't, but I wanted her to have peace after eight days of worrying. Purple half-moons rested under her tired eyes, and her normally fluffy hair was flat and tucked behind her ears. She looked like I felt. I didn't even see my dad until I felt his meaty hand on my shoulder and turned my head. Shooting pains accompanied with yellow spots filled my vision, and I closed my eyes. I heard my mom gasp.

"Can you give her something for the pain?" My mom's voice was laced with panic.

"Definitely. I'll have something sent in right away. Sawyer, I'm leaving for the night, but I'll be back in the morning. Your job is to get as much sleep as you can because tomorrow we're going to get you up and out of bed," Macey said.

I couldn't imagine doing anything but sleeping, but I humored her with a weak, one-handed thumbs-up. "Sounds good."

"Your family has been with you around the clock. Enjoy the night, but make sure you sleep," Macey said. She leaned over me with her penlight to check my pupil response and my mouth dropped open when a tiny ladybug on a silver chain dangled away from her neck in the narrow space between us. Fuck. It was all starting to fall into place, and the reality was devastating.

❖

"Wait, what?"

I was sitting up in the hospital bed after my first shower since I woke up two days ago. It took two nurses and a lot of sweating on my part to make it happen, but I needed to be clean. I was tired of smelling dried blood, sweat, and tears. "Google Ladybug Junction. Tell me if it's a real town in Alabama." I knew the answer already, but the sliver of hope I held on to crashed at my feet when I saw Macey's necklace. I watched as Tamsyn scrolled on her phone and shook her head.

"Lots of businesses named that, but no town." She put her phone down and focused on me. "So, when you were in a coma—"

I interrupted. "Medically induced."

"Still coma," she said.

I shrugged.

"So, you dreamed your doctor was a librarian and y'all had sex?" she asked.

"Shh!" I looked around to see if any of the nurses were

within earshot. "That's a quick summary, but yes. Like, I can't explain it. This hospital room was her bedroom in her house. I remember the flowers and how they smelled. Same name, same woman, but she was a librarian, not a doctor. I'm so confused."

Tamsyn held my hand. "They say sometimes you can hear people in comas. I wonder if your senses picked up things subconsciously?"

I dropped my head back on my pillow and sighed. "I want to talk to somebody."

"What about hot doc? I'm sure this happens all the time. She probably has answers or can send you to somebody who has them. Listen, you are not the first person who's experienced this. We hear about this kind of thing on documentaries. Has Dr. Burr been in today?"

"No. I think it's her day off. But there are other doctors who might be able to explain it. The last thing I want is to tell her that we hooked up in my dream."

Tamsyn carefully lifted my hair to look at the sutures. "Now you'll have a story to go with this scar," she said.

"I'd rather not have either." I was starting to get cabin fever, and even though all my tests came back normal, they were going to keep me an extra day. They wanted me to walk on my own and eat solids before they released me. I also had to sign up for physical therapy. It was a lot.

"Scars are sexy," Tamsyn said.

I looked at my hairline in the compact mirror Tamsyn handed me. At least the nurses were able to wash the blood out of my hair. I had it pulled back in a ponytail so they could redress the sutures easier.

"I feel and smell so much better." I lifted my bulky cast. "At least it's removable. I can't imagine the next five weeks without a proper bath or shower."

"I'll bring you a robe tonight," Tamsyn said. At the crushed look on my face, she quickly added, "But you'll only need it for one night. What clothes do you want me to bring from home?

Definitely your cute pink sweats and maybe something that's easy to slip into like my zip-up UCLA sweatshirt?"

"That sounds great." Tamsyn was five foot ten. I swam in her clothes, but that sounded so comforting. I nodded, then groaned. Shit. What was I going to wear to go to work? And how was I going to work for the next two or so months? I couldn't do animal physicals or even pick up a pet.

"Does Oliver know I'm here? Has work reached out?" I asked.

Tamsyn pointed to a large bouquet on the windowsill. A few flowers were wilting, but somebody had done a nice job of pruning out the dead ones. "They sent these the moment I told them. Oliver sounded very concerned."

I scoffed and rolled my eyes. "He's probably worried I'm going to sue since I was on company time." Honestly, I didn't remember how or why I crashed. Macey told me what happened, but it felt like it happened to somebody else. Tamsyn showed me photos of my car, and the fact that I was carted away with only a broken elbow, bruises, and stitches was amazing.

"Oh, stop. They care about you." She looked at me and we both laughed. "Okay, let's take the time off work to look into opening up your own practice."

I held up my cast and looked at her like she was bonkers.

"What? You're not dead. You have a busted elbow. You can still fill out paperwork and look at places. The process will take months, so we have time. You'll be healed by the time you open the doors."

Her idea had merit. What was I going to do at the office? The assistants filled out paperwork. I could hang around to consult, but how many times would they need me? I shook my head. I was getting way ahead of myself. "Let's focus on breaking me out of here."

"You're on solids, right?" she asked.

"I'm supposed to get eggs and oatmeal this morning." I

checked the clock. It was almost seven thirty. "You need to get to work. I'm sure my mom's going to be here soon."

Tamsyn kissed my cheek. "I'll see you tonight. Lauren and Arya want to swing by. So, look for us with fresh clothes tonight after work."

Her eyes watered up and I pointed at her. She held her hand up. "You look so much better today. And smell better, too."

"Thanks. I'll see you all tonight." I watched her leave and make a face when a cute hospitalist slipped into my room with a tray of food. She gave me a quick thumbs-up before the door fully closed.

"Good morning, Ms. Noel. I'm Britt and I have eggs, oatmeal, toast, fruit, orange juice, and coffee for you." She pulled the tray over and hit the button to raise the bed. "Do you need me to call for a nurse to help?"

I waved her off because I felt stronger and I needed to do things on my own or else I would never get out of here. "I'm good. It's just taking me a bit of time to adjust." I held up my elbow and smiled.

"Well, let me know if you need anything. Anything at all." The tiny smile on her face made me light up. She was obviously too young for me and probably said that to everyone, but it felt good.

"Thank you. I appreciate it." I waited until she was out of the room before I tried to pick up my fork. I was still weak, but damn it, I was hungry and wanted to go home. I reached for the toast instead. It was dry, but it was delicious and the loud crunch made me smile. I missed chewing. The bite stung my raw throat, but solid food tasted good. I reached for a piece of fruit right when Macey walked in. I froze before putting a strawberry in my mouth. "Hi. I didn't think you were working today." My voice was still raspy, but I felt a ton better since my shower. I put the strawberry back in the bowl and discreetly wiped my fingers on the napkin in my lap. She pulled a chair closer to my bedside.

"I heard you had a good night. I wanted to check in with you. The next twenty-four hours are going to be whirlwind, but you'll have the opportunity to go home soon."

I froze when she leaned over me to look at my sutures.

"And these are healing nicely." She was still leaning over me when she looked into my eyes and asked me my pain level.

"My headache is only a dull throb. My elbow is bulky and annoying, but it doesn't hurt."

"Are you getting around okay?" she asked.

"I use the crutch and sweat out every single calorie to get to the bathroom, but I can do it. The shower felt amazing."

"You look so much better. People heal faster when they're home. After your evaluation from the rest of the team, I can almost guarantee you'll be released tomorrow. Do you have any questions for me?"

She smelled like she did in my dream. "I'm not sure how to ask this, but do people hear things when they're in a coma?"

She nodded. "There's strong evidence that people can hear, smell, and feel things when they are in a coma. Did you experience something?"

It was now or never. I wanted answers, but I didn't want to freak her out. I chose my words carefully. "I recognize your voice and some of your characteristics, but it felt more like I was in a dream." Well, that wasn't true. "I mean, it felt like it was real." I liked how she gave me her undivided attention. It was unnerving to tell her what happened, but also important for me to share my story. "In this dream world, my electric car ran out of charge and kind of coasted into this small town. You were there and helped me." Even as I was saying the words, it was starting to fall into place. "Was that my brain protecting me from what really happened to me?" I asked.

"The brain is an amazing organ that oversees everything in your body and will protect you when something traumatic like this happens. It is completely possible outside influences were affecting your mind. Can you tell me more?" she asked.

It felt ridiculous to say the words out loud, but I took a deep breath and told her the story. "You were a librarian in a small town and your aunt had a quaint inn with a really impressive garden." I looked around my room and realized the twelve bouquets of flowers gave the room an almost sickeningly sweet smell. "Probably the flowers in my room." I felt my shoulders sink as the reality around me answered my questions, but then I remembered one thing that didn't fit and looked at her neck. "The name of the town was Ladybug Junction. You're wearing a necklace with a ladybug. How could I have seen that if I was in a coma?" I felt her warm hand on mine and looked up at her.

"I'm going to guess that's because you were fading in and out of consciousness when you first arrived. I was called in to evaluate you. Maybe you saw my necklace that morning and everything slipped into place for you," she said. She pulled out her identification and headed for the computer. "If you want, I can add a few visits with a therapist who might be able to help you understand things better. I highly recommend her. She's done wonders for several of my patients." She typed a few things into my file before locking up and returning to my bedside. She was close, and it was hard not to react in any way other than a patient would with her doctor.

"I'm glad you stopped by," I said.

She leaned back. My vibe was intense, so I relaxed.

"I'm glad you're doing better. You gave us all quite a scare." It seemed like she wanted to say more but squeezed my hand and stood instead. "Enjoy your breakfast. I'll be back to check on you this afternoon."

"Thank you, Dr. Burr." I stumbled over her name because I wanted to call her Macey. I wanted to hold her hand and pull her closer and tell her I'd call her later, but it was wrong. My reality was screwed up and a big part of me wanted to go back to a place that didn't exist.

CHAPTER SIX

D r. Burr. How are you?" I was early for my therapy session and swung by the hospital's café to pick up a coffee. It had been three weeks since I was released. I was getting to the point where I didn't need my cast full-time but only wore a sling. My at-home physical therapy exercises were working. Today I was at the hospital to meet with my therapist, Kerri Rivers, to work through the events before and after my wreck. I almost didn't say anything to Macey, but I had to walk by her to get to the coffee station.

"Ms. Noel. You look like you're healing nicely." She gave me a full up and down. "How are you doing?" She pointed to my sling. I brushed off the ding to my ego because I thought she liked my overall look. My hair was styled over the scar on my forehead, my makeup was fresh, and I looked human again.

"Call me Sawyer, please. I feel good. My elbow throbs from time to time, but I'm on the mend." In a move that surprised me, she pointed to the chair opposite her.

"Do you have time to chat?" she asked.

Even if I didn't, I was going to sit down.

"Sure. Can I grab a cup of coffee?" She waved off my offer to get her another one, so I quickly poured a cup and joined her at the table.

"How's therapy?" she asked.

I wasn't sure which one she meant since I had two therapists. "I'm no longer required to wear my cast all day, so that's amazing. Driving is challenging, but overall, I'm sitting at about a seven on a scale of one to ten. I'm meeting with Kerri today."

"First session?" she asked.

I stirred a sugar packet into my coffee and tried to not spill everything. "Third. The first session was just an introduction discussing what I wanted out of therapy. She gave me an assignment for session two. I think we're headed in the right direction," I said.

Tamsyn was right. A lot of people heard and smelled things while in comas. After only one session, it was clear that my brain was working out a lot of stresses. Kerri asked me to keep a journal of people and events from Ladybug Junction and how they related to the real world. That would be my starting point. We could tackle each subject to see what was really going on or if it was just my brain doing its job. Obviously, I was attracted to Macey, and she was the first person I wanted to discuss. All of it was unsettling, but it felt good to talk about it. Some of the people in Ladybug Junction didn't have obvious tethers to the real world, but Kerri seemed confident that we would figure them out. Voices were familiar, and beeps from my monitoring equipment and ventilator wormed their way into dream world. Even the smells were sharp. Separating the two was my first goal. The second was understanding why I was so fixated on Macey the librarian, not Macey the doctor. It was going to be a long road ahead.

"I knew she'd be helpful," she said. She checked her watch and I saw her shoulders relax. Apparently, she had more time to spare. I had about eight minutes before I was late but had no plans to leave.

"How's neurology going?" I asked. It was a stupid question, but I didn't know how to get into a conversation with her. Her laugh was delightful.

"There's always something fascinating about it. I'm learning new things every day."

Her smile was bright and confident, but the Macey in front of me wasn't as bubbly as the Macey from my dreamlike state. She was quiet, reserved, but just as lovely. It occurred to me that I didn't know if Dr. Macey Burr was even a lesbian. Her hands were void of any jewelry, but I noticed a lot of doctors and nurses didn't wear rings because they were constantly putting on and tearing off gloves.

"And you love it so much, you come in on your days off," I said.

"Well, I was concerned about my patient."

I blushed. "Thank you. I feel a hundred times better. My stitches are out and my bruises are almost gone." I moved my arm away from my body. "It'll only be a few more weeks before my elbow is fully healed. So, thank you." I weirdly tapped her hand and pulled back.

"Well, it's my job, but I'm happy to hear you're doing so well. Are you able to work?" she asked. Her eyes looked tired, but she seemed laser focused.

"They call me in for consultations, but mostly I sit around the house and watch movies or listen to audiobooks. I'm completely bored." This Macey didn't need to know that I was in the process of considering starting my own business. It was difficult remembering what she knew versus what I thought I told her.

"Hopefully, physical therapy will get you back up and handling pets in no time."

I missed the relationship we had in my dream state. I had a lot of questions for Kerri, and she was helping me weed through the web of my thoughts, but it was going to take time. "Do you have any pets?" She gave me a peculiar look and I feared I asked the question already and forgot. I tapped my temple. "I'm still trying to separate truth from fiction, so I'm sorry if you've told me and I don't remember. That's why I have a meeting in..." I looked at my phone. "Three minutes."

She raised her eyebrows. "You'd better get going so you're not late."

I didn't want to go. I missed the spark between us and had been searching for it since I woke up. I had a lot of questions for Kerri, though, and the sooner we worked through my mental healing process, the sooner I could fill in the gaps. "It's been nice catching up. Maybe we could do it again? Outside of these four walls?" Since I was already standing, I could make a quick getaway if she turned me down.

"As nice as that would be, fraternizing with my patients is unethical. But thank you for the invitation."

She sounded so proper, but more importantly, interested. Shit, two minutes.

"Are you always going to be my doctor?"

She crossed her arms in front of her chest and gave me a smirk. "Unless you request another doctor for follow-ups, you're stuck with me."

I knocked on the tabletop with my knuckle. "You'll be hearing from me, Doc." With as much coolness as I could muster, I turned and walked toward the elevator.

❖

Tamsyn's fingers felt strong on my shoulders as her eyes bored into mine. "Look, I'm so happy you are up and moving and things are going well, but I'm super confused about what's happening. You quit Dr. Burr so you can see her. That doesn't even make sense."

I waited until my words sank in. Tamsyn didn't disappoint. Her blue eyes widened, and her mouth opened in surprise.

"Shut up. Really?"

I shrugged. "Maybe it's a mistake. She said it would be unethical to see me outside of the hospital as my physician, so I transferred my case to another neurologist. My next appointment is a three-month checkup, so it's not even an issue."

Tamsyn howled with laughter and slapped her hand on her knee. "That's amazing. Now what happens?"

I had Macey's private phone number on the back of her business card. "I guess I call her and invite her out to dinner."

Tamsyn groaned. "That's boring. What does she like to do?"

I shot her a look. "You're asking the impossible question."

"Still working that part out with your therapist?" she asked.

"I've had three sessions. We're just now scratching the surface." I liked how Kerri was guiding me toward answers but letting me figure things out for myself. It still blew my mind that I hadn't gone to a therapist before.

"I guess dinner is probably the best bet. Take her to that new farm-to-table restaurant that just opened in Parkview Heights. Lauren went with her boss and they loved it," Tamsyn said. At my look, she pulled up the website. "Don't worry. It's not long wooden tables in an outdoor tent." She handed me her phone. "See? Fine dining. Linen napkins, candles, romantic vibe. I dig it. Hey, maybe we should check it out first. Why don't I try to make reservations for this week?"

Tamsyn's tongue peeked out from her lips while she concentrated on dates and times. I was lucky to have her in my life. She'd been at my side through every horrible experience. She caught me gazing at her.

"You're doing that thing again."

"I love you," I said.

"You love me because I gave you a sponge bath."

I threw my head back and laughed. "You helped me dress. No sponge was involved. I love you because you're the best."

"I am, right?" She threw a paper straw at me. "So, dinner Wednesday night?" She held up her finger and yelled to Lauren in the other room. "Do we have plans on Wednesday? Can we find a babysitter and eat at Oak Barrel?" I knew Lauren nodded from the smile that broke out on Tamsyn's face.

"Okay, dinner at seven. And if you like it, call Doc for a date."

The thought of calling her made my stomach flip. I still didn't know if she was interested in me. Our conversation was vague enough to encourage me, but murky enough to make an ass of me if she said no. Good news. If she said no, we'd never run into each other again. "Sounds good. I'll see you there?"

"We'll pick you up," she said.

It was hard to drive with an elbow in a sling, but not impossible. I was appreciative that they offered. After my accident and totaling my car, I needed new wheels. I picked a Subaru Crosstrek hybrid. Therapy told me I stressed too much about a fully electric car, so I decided on something in-between. I hadn't driven it much, but it was nice to have transportation and I was getting great mileage.

"Have you looked at the names yet?" Tamsyn asked.

She was referring to a list of about fifty possible business names she emailed me this morning. It was overwhelming. I had a business plan, but I was still interviewing banks and trying to find the ideal location. Tamsyn found a small building near her campus that seemed perfect, but I was looking for something closer to home. "Not yet. It's kind of overwhelming."

"You should call it something with the word 'paws.' Like Paws and Claws or Awesome Pawsome. Something that tells people you're a veterinarian, but that you're not boring like Oliver Strong."

Her idea had merit although I wasn't looking for whimsical. "Perfect Paws."

Tamsyn shot it down. "Sounds like a dog grooming place."

I slowly nodded. "Sawyer Noel…" I said.

She held up her hand to stop me. "Nope. Boring. Don't be like Oliver."

I chewed my bottom lip until I had a halfway decent name. "How about Healing Paws?"

"That's not horrible. It's light but tells people exactly what your business is. And Lauren can come up with a cute logo and design," she said. She leaned so far back in her chair that the front two legs were off the floor. "Honey? Can you come in here?" She landed with a thud. "You know Lauren will be truthful."

"What's going on?"

Lauren put her hands on Tamsyn's shoulders and kissed her cheek. They were the dream couple.

"What do you think of Healing Paws or Healthy Paws for a business name?" Tamsyn asked.

"It's better than Oliver Strong, DMV. You can still have your name as a subheading if you really want it." Lauren held her hand out and moved it six inches with every word as though she was reading a marquee. "Healing Paws." She moved down to an imaginary line below it. "Sawyer Noel, DMV." She dropped her hand. "And we can make your name smaller. You can have cute little paw prints. Let me mock something up and get it to you this week."

Things were going faster than I imagined. I knew Lauren would do a good job. I just needed to pull the trigger, give Oliver my notice, and focus on me. Nothing like a car crash and a coma to put life into perspective.

"You'll have all the women rushing to your practice. You know I'll put in a good word with my staff and put something on the university's intranet when you open. I'm so excited for this," Tamsyn said.

"I'm so nervous. It's a lot of money and a big commitment." I wasn't worried about getting customers. I was worried about getting a good staff. I was fearful that Oliver would bad-mouth me to existing customers and veterinarians in the area who might be looking. I was going to have to leave on the best possible terms, but even then, there wasn't a guarantee that he or evil Meredith wouldn't speak ill of me. I also had my sights on poaching Yara, the best technician we had on staff. If I got her to work for me, they would for sure talk shit. Crap. They were going to be jerks no matter what. Tamsyn saw the scowl on my face and assumed I was having second thoughts.

"You've got this. You have the support of us and our friends. We'll have a huge grand opening party with a best pet costume contest, puppy race, rodent maze race, and other weird things. I'm sure you'll get some ideas from this weekend."

She was referring to our free pop-up clinic near the farmer's market on Saturday. Oliver Strong Clinic had a tent set up where we offered free rabies shots, free microchipping, pet dental care, low-cost supplies, free toys, and free dog baths. I supported the team when they approached Oliver with the idea, but now I was worried that I wasn't going to be able to do a lot. I was still in a sling, and no way could I wrangle upset or scared animals. My participation was limited, and that was disappointing to the entire office. They expected me to do most of the work, but with a busted elbow, Oliver or Meredith would have to step up. "I don't even know how well that's going to go."

"Surely, Meredith can give shots and stuff, right? I mean, she's still a doctor."

I wasn't giving my nemesis enough credit. This was right up her alley. "You're right. She'll nail it. I'll pass out toys or something." Oliver had tennis balls, Frisbees, and squeaky toys with our name and phone number printed on them. Correction, with his name printed on it. Tamsyn was right. It was better to have a name that felt light and safe. Healing Paws, the one I was leaning toward, was a bit hokey, but it would look better on a toy or a magnet than just my name. "Okay, I'm headed home. Thanks for everything and the awesome pep talk."

"Don't overdo it. You have a long week ahead," Tamsyn said.

She was right. It was only Monday and I was exhausted. I put in a full day at work, which meant I sat in my tiny office, signed papers, ordered supplies, and begged to see patients. I missed helping. I missed Snoops the beagle who suffered from seizures, and Benny the cat who got in a fight and needed stitches in his ear, and I even missed Princess, a fluffy Pomeranian who was one hundred percent healthy, but her elderly owner was extremely lonely and wanted to talk to people about her precious dog. It was a win-win. I got snuggles and Princess's owner spent an hour talking to the staff. I hated that Oliver took money from her every week. Maybe Healing Paws could have a small gated area for playdates, and Princess and other dogs could play and her owner could find other people who loved to talk about their pets as much as she did. I wouldn't charge them. I could call it Playdate Park where people scheduled time and we could make it a fun affair. The idea was starting to take root, and even though the thought of going out on my own was scary, I was pumped about the ideas that were a vast improvement over my current working situation. I was going to nail it.

CHAPTER SEVEN

"Can you please look at my hedgehog? He's finicky and might need a shot or something."

I was organizing toys by size and looked up to find Macey standing in front of me empty-handed. "I'm sorry, but did you just make fun of your coma patient?" I tried hard not to smile but she looked horrified at a joke she thought fell flat. I gave her a swift wink.

She recovered nicely. "But you're not my patient anymore."

I held it together a second before I busted out laughing. "Fair. What are you doing here?" My heart felt light at seeing her standing in front of me in shorts and a cute pale blue top. Her hair was braided back and slung over her shoulder. She didn't look like the doctor with stress lines on her forehead and the corners of her mouth pinched downward who peered into my eyes with a penlight several times a day for a week. No, the woman in front of me looked relaxed and carefree and more like the woman from my dream world.

"Well, you've seen me in action, so I thought I'd return the favor," she said.

I lifted my arm away from my body and waved it as though she couldn't see my sling. I opted for the removable cast today because I knew that without it, I would try to do too much and might aggravate my injury. "What a nice surprise, but the only action you're going to see is me playing with pet toys and wishing I could help more." I was hiding in the corner and sulking because Meredith was killing it with patients and visitors. I wasn't needed as much as I thought I would be.

Macey turned to survey the action around us and I quickly gave her a once-over. Her legs were tanned and toned, and her body was fit. She hid her form well under her doctor's white coat that covered her curves. She struck me as somebody who did yoga, ate organic food, and avoided sugar.

"Looks like an amazing turnout," she said.

"It's been steady all morning." I hated that I was in a corner awkwardly sifting through boxes of toys instead of treating and smooching the animals visiting our booth. I wanted her to see me in my element, but instead, she caught me trying to one-hand juggle catnip mice.

"Do you get a lunch break?" she asked.

I would have given Oliver my two-week notice had he said no to breaks. "I'm sure I can get away for lunch or coffee."

She pointed to a small bistro down the street with outdoor tables. "How about there?"

I didn't want everyone I work with watching me, but I also didn't want to say no to Macey. "Sounds great."

I told Oliver I was taking a break and hoped everyone wasn't watching us leave. Macey was the kind of woman who turned heads. From her thick, wavy blond hair to her flawless skin, I knew all my coworkers' eyes were on her. I was covered in dog hair, smelled like animals, and wore khaki pants and a polo shirt with Oliver's name on it. My hair was pulled back in a ponytail and I had sweated off my makeup. I was the proverbial hot mess, but I didn't care. I was spending time with Macey outside of the hospital.

"Do you get weekends off?" I asked. I lost track of time in the hospital.

She shook her head. "I schedule the occasional weekend off

if it's important. Most of my off days are random throughout the week."

"Oh, this must be an important weekend. What's going on?" I couldn't believe I was so chill when my pulse was fluttering at an alarming rate.

"I know it sounds childish, but it's my birthday and I wanted a day to unwind. Maybe have a glass of wine and enjoy fresh air."

I touched her arm. "How perfect. Happy birthday."

She moved a fraction closer. "It's silly, I know," she said.

"Not at all. We don't take enough time for ourselves as adults. Do you have plans? Family get-together later? Date night?" Who was I to ask her such personal questions? "I mean, it's an important day."

She shrugged. "This is it. A trip to the farmer's market and picking up some fresh flowers." She held up the bouquet of red and pink gerber daisies. "I like simple things. My work's complicated, so this is how I like to unwind."

"No kayaking or bike riding?" The Macey I remembered was all about outdoor adventure and nature hikes.

"That's not really my thing, plus it's hard to make time for that. I'm on call a lot," she said. "But I have a Peloton and a treadmill to stay in shape." She took a deep breath. "So, you can understand why I wanted to be outside today."

"I get it. We'll celebrate it over salads and wine." I wasn't sure I was going to drink, given I was on the clock. To be fair, my expertise needed today extended to what was the best flea treatment for sensitive skin and what over-the-counter allergy medication a dog could take. I doubted one glass of wine would make me forget a decade of education combined with applied experience.

The oversized umbrella shaded us from the late summer heat. I excused myself to wash up and check my appearance after we placed our order. I had a slight sunburn on my face and some dog hair on my polo, but I didn't look bad. I washed my hands, pressed my khakis flat, and weaved my way to the front where Macey sat. I slid onto the chair and drank the ice water in front of me.

"It's nice to see you away from your job. I hope I didn't hurt your feelings when I switched doctors." I interlocked my fingers the best I could in my cumbersome cast and leaned on the table. It put me in her personal space, and she didn't move. That was a good sign.

"The raving review you left me made up for my hurt feelings," she said. Her eyes were bright in the natural light. Flecks of brown, green, and a ring of blue made them unique. Out here, in the sunshine, the blue dominated. A smile perched on her full lips, and it was hard not to stare. She was gorgeous and seemingly unaware that she had the attention of several patrons.

"Come on. All your patients give you five-star reviews, right?"

"About ninety-nine percent of the time. I've only had two patients request a different doctor," she said.

"Including me?" At her nod, I frowned. "Does that hurt you as a doctor in any way?" I was concerned about her reputation and my plan backfiring.

"Not at all. As a matter of fact, let's just say I'm glad you did."

"Oh?" This conversation was going exactly in the direction I wanted. I cocked my head and smiled. Was my dream girl interested in me?

"It's nice to be able to spend time with someone on my birthday."

I couldn't tell if she was purposely teasing me or if she thought of me only as a new friend. "Let me take you out on a real date for your birthday. I mean this is nice, but how about dinner somewhere where they serve quality wine and delicious food? Plus, it gives me time to clean up and not smell like a dog." I wrinkled my nose playfully and hoped she'd say yes.

"I'm very boring," she said.

I shook my head. "Not a deterrent and I don't believe you, but if you don't want to, I completely understand." I speared a tomato and popped it in my mouth, waiting for her answer, hoping I wasn't going to choke if she said no.

"Dinner sounds nice."

I swallowed after I processed her answer. It gave me time to squelch the shout of excitement. "Great. Have you been to Oak Barrel?" I asked.

Her smile hinted at sadness. "I can't tell you the last time I went to dinner. Or when my last date was." She leaned back in her chair and sipped her wine.

"You work a lot of hours. How many patients do you have?"

"That's a tough question. Around a dozen a day. I have a lot of follow-ups and consultations."

"What made you want to become a neurologist?" I was genuinely curious as to why people picked specific careers. I had a soft spot for animals and knew I wanted to be a veterinarian since high school. My parents always wanted me to go to medical school and I did, only not the kind that specialized in humans. I still made good money and considered myself successful.

"One of my aunts fell out of a roller coaster when I was young. She survived but had head trauma. Watching her relearn motor skills and learn how to do basic functions like walk and talk again was inspiring. She never gave up or lost hope. The brain is a remarkable organ. Even when it's severely damaged, it tries to do its job."

Well, I had a zillion questions and was completely invested in her aunt's story. "How is your aunt now?"

"She still struggles and can't do some of the things we take for granted like drive a car or carry an armful of groceries, but she's happy and thankful she's alive. So, when patients like yourself have head trauma, we don't know how extensive the injury is until you're conscious."

"I was lucky. And had a great doctor," I said. I knew I was laying it on kind of thick. She grew quiet and I thought I pushed it too far. "Your aunt sounds like an amazing woman. Does she live around here?" I asked.

"About twenty minutes away. My whole family lives in town. Aunt Abby lives next door to my parents. As a matter of fact, I bought these flowers for her. I'm going to see her this afternoon."

I sat there stunned. Aunt Abby. Aunt Abby. Same person. How the fuck did I already know about Aunt Abby? I tried to stay focused on Macey, but it was hard, as thoughts from my dream world and the real world collided. She kept talking while I nibbled on lettuce, sipped on ice water, and processed what she said without completely freaking out. "That sounds like a great idea. Are daisies her favorite?"

"She loves all flowers really, but red and pink are her favorite colors." She touched the bouquet and smiled. "What's your favorite flower?"

Thoughts scattered in my brain like a game of hide-and-seek, and for the life of me, I couldn't come up with my favorite flower. I couldn't find my words. I couldn't tell her that I loved tulips because they were one of the first flowers to bloom every year and were simple and lovely. Instead, I shrugged and said, "I don't know."

"Really?" she asked. She leaned her arm on the back of her chair. The move stretched her shirt tight across her breasts. I stared directly in her eyes, but my peripheral vision picked up nice curves and the outline of a lacy bra.

I took a deep breath and found my words. "I guess my favorite is the tulip."

"Those are pretty. I love seeing the tulip fields people post on Instagram," Macey said.

The fact that she had time for social media surprised me. Macey didn't strike me as the kind of person who scrolled in between appointments. "You're on Instagram?"

She put her hand on her chest—a move that drew my attention back to her breasts. This time I looked. "Secretly, it's the only one I'm on. I avoid all the others because they suck all my spare time and I'd rather use it to visit my family."

I blushed because I spent hours a day on social media, especially since work was hard, so I killed time on at least five platforms.

"It's a great way for me to decompress. Most of my wall is National Geographic, wildlife refuges, and kittens," she said.

"Same. Plus, I follow Tamsyn and my mom. My mom's surprisingly savvy for being in her sixties," I said.

Macey's phone rang before I could ask her about her mother. She held up a finger and turned her body to the side to take the call. I checked the time and realized we'd been sitting for an hour. Where did the time go?

"Speak of the devil, that was my aunt. Apparently, I'm late," Macey said. She waved over the waiter to pay the check.

"I didn't realize the time either. About tonight, do you want me to pick you up?" It had been so long since I had my last first date I wasn't sure if offering to pick her up was offensive or the right thing to do.

"Why don't you let me pick you up since you're still in a cast, or we can meet there."

I'd forgotten about my cast. I sheepishly looked at it and shrugged. "Why don't we just meet there at seven? Does that give you enough time with your aunt?"

She stood and picked up her flowers and shopping bag. "That's perfect. I'll see you later tonight." She surprised me by giving me a quick hug. I didn't have time to steel myself and I almost moaned at how soft she felt.

"I'm looking forward to it." I allowed myself two seconds to watch her walk away, then I quickly headed back to the tent. I had a lot to process, but I also had to get back to work. "Did I miss anything?" I slid next to Yara, who was adding names to a mailing list.

She smiled. "Same, steady flow. You missed a cute bulldog puppy, two tabby kittens, the most adorable little boy with a lizard. Oh, and somewhere around here is a baby goat from the sanctuary. But that's not important right now." She nudged my good arm with her elbow. "How was your date with the hottie?"

I could feel the flame on my cheeks. "Oh, you saw that, huh?"

"We all saw it and we have questions." She waved over Tyler, who was organizing the last of the free toys.

"I don't have answers yet. Ask me on Monday and maybe I'll have a story to tell." I didn't have any intentions of telling them about the date, but our camaraderie felt authentic and I was totally in the moment.

CHAPTER EIGHT

Macey was already seated when I arrived. Her dress was sapphire blue with a square neckline. Her hair was scooped up in the back and small tendrils framed her face. The candlelight gave a warm, ethereal glow and I was stunned by her beauty. I was in the sweet, special moment where I could look at Macey because I was there for her and not worry about getting caught blatantly staring. She was breathtaking.

"Can I help you?" The hostess of the restaurant slid in the space between me and Macey.

I frowned at the invasion. I pointed at Macey. "My date is already here. The reservation is under Noel."

Maybe she did it to piss me off, but she made me wait until she reviewed the reservation list. "Sawyer?"

I nodded and blinked rapidly several times. She did the same. "Sawyer," I repeated firmly. I sidestepped the hostess and made my way over to our table and was greeted with another swift hug.

Macey's voice floated over the soft chatter of people and made me instantly smile. "How's the elbow?" she asked.

I slid into the chair opposite her and bent my arm up and down. "It's great. I'm happy I wore the cast during the event today, though." I touched her hand. "You look amazing."

"Thank you. So do you," she said.

I decided on a simple, sleeveless black dress that hit above the knee. For the first time in forever, I felt sexy. Tamsyn fixed my hair because lifting my arm above my head to style it was exhausting. Plus, she wanted to pump me up and get me excited about my date, but that wasn't necessary. I was already almost floating. "What are you drinking?"

She held up a glass of red wine. "A merlot. I've been here for about fifteen minutes."

I waited in my car for ten minutes so that I was only five minutes early. "Blue is a great color on you." I didn't disguise my appreciation. Her words finally sank in. Had we agreed on a different time? "Wait. Am I late?"

She shook her head. "Not at all. I just had nothing else to do."

I found that hard to believe, but I went along. Maybe Macey was the kind of person who literally stepped away from work on her day off or it consumed her. "Well, thank you for letting me celebrate your birthday with you. I'm guessing thirty?" Her laugh was delightful.

"A little higher."

I raised my eyebrow at her. She really wasn't going to tell me. "Where did you go to school?" I was hoping she would tell me the year she graduated so I could quickly do the math, but her information didn't help me.

"I went to Emory for undergraduate and medical school."

"Impressive. I went to Iowa State. It was tough being away from home, and the Midwest isn't the greatest place for queers, but I had a full ride and it was hard to say no."

"I get it. Student loans are a bitch," she said.

We were interrupted by a waiter who rattled off the specials so fast that I asked him to repeat them. It was hard to tear my attention away from Macey. "I'll have the wood smoked salmon and a glass of the 2021 Sauvignon Blanc."

She ordered the gnocchi and a fresh glass of wine. "How are your parents?" Macey asked.

"They're doing well. Very happy I made it out alive and in one piece."

"Your friend and your parents took turns staying in your room the entire time. It was touching to see."

That confused me. "Do people normally not do that?"

She shrugged. "It's hard to tell how long somebody is going to be in a coma. Yours was controlled and we knew you'd wake up within a few hours."

"That was without a doubt the worst I've ever felt. I can't imagine understanding what some patients who have been in comas for months have to deal with." Recalling the pain and confusion made me shudder.

"You got banged up pretty bad, but I have to say, you clean up nicely," Macey said.

I blushed and took a sip of wine. The feelings that swirled inside me felt fresh and light. I'd forgotten what it was like to have a conversation with a beautiful woman who was positive and complimentary and real. "Thank you for all your help and all your time."

"I'd say I was just doing my job, but I was invested in you. I mean, in your case."

"I'm sure you have very interesting stories. It must be fascinating studying the brain." I was still trying to process my experience. And the story about her aunt? I wanted more details but it was rude to ask.

"I've written several papers and I know I've only scratched the surface. I'll spend my entire career trying to learn as much as I can and will probably only find out a fraction."

"I think that's fascinating," I said. It was only fair to come clean about the one thing I didn't tell her about my coma experience. "Speaking of fascinating, there's something I think I need to tell you."

She leaned forward and smiled. "Oh?"

I felt a slow growing heat crawl up my neck and splash across my cheeks. It didn't go unnoticed.

"Wow. This must be good," she said.

"So, when I was in my dream world, you and I…" I paused because maybe this would jeopardize the rest of the night and any possible future relationship with Macey.

"You can tell me." She rested her hand on mine and gave it an encouraging squeeze.

Here went nothing. "We were dating." I shrugged like it was no big deal, but my heart was racing in anticipation of her response. I was expecting her to pull away and be freaked out, but she gave me a half smile. "Obviously, nothing serious, but I needed to tell you that."

"It's interesting that you assumed I was queer in your dream world," she said.

"Right? I mean, two for two. I should go play the lottery or something." I tried to joke my way out of my uncomfortableness, but she was gracious and understanding.

"That's actually pretty funny," she said.

"Okay, confession over. Now I'm embarrassed. Let's talk about something else. Let's talk about you. I know why you became a neurologist. What's the best part of your job?"

"I love helping people. I'm sure you know exactly what I mean. I feel like you know all about me. Let's talk more about you. What's new with you?"

"The most exciting thing is that I'm for sure going to open my own practice." Had I told her this? Were any of the conversations about this with her in the real world? Her warm fingers squeezed mine and lingered. I looked down at her perfectly manicured fingers and brazenly linked them with mine.

"That's so exciting. Good for you. How far in the process are you?" she asked.

I studied her face for any signs that she was only humoring me, but she seemed genuinely interested in my life. "I've visited a few banks and I'm still trying to find the perfect location, but I think I'm pretty close to talking to my boss."

"If I had a pet, I would definitely be a patron of yours."

"We can always find you one," I said.

She waved me off. "Oh no. I work too many hours to give a pet a good home. I can just show up and be the office cuddler."

I smiled. Regrettably, we stopped holding hands when the food arrived. I explained my business idea over the first few bites. By the time we finished dessert, she knew my plan and strongly encouraged me to pursue my dream. "I feel so bad. I did all the talking."

"I love it. You're so excited and I know it's going to be successful. You have so much passion for your practice," she said.

We were so into the conversation that the waiter startled us when he dropped the check on the table in front of us. I put my hand on it first. "It's your birthday and my invitation." She held her hands up and gave me a small nod.

"That's fair," she said.

I slipped my card in the plastic holder. "I don't want tonight to end just yet." It was nine thirty and I was nowhere ready to call it a night. "I mean, unless you need to go. I'm sure you have a busy day tomorrow."

She stood. "How about a nightcap?"

Her voice was smooth, and the implication made my knees weak. I put my hand on the table to steady myself. "That sounds great." I tried to keep the excitement from my voice and gave her a sweet smile instead. "Do you know a good place?"

She grabbed her clutch. "My place is only about ten minutes away."

Every part of my body twitched. I wasn't expecting anything other than dinner, but hope blossomed at the thought of something more like kissing her full lips or my hands on her soft curves. "I'm right behind you."

I watched her slip into a Lexus coupe and followed her to a very nice, gated community about five miles from the restaurant.

My stomach quivered when I put my car in park and met her at the front door. "Nice house," I said.

"Thank you. Come on in. I'll give you a quick tour."

I lived in a condo. It wasn't my forever home, but Macey's house was one where you raised a family and retired comfortably. To say it was spacious was an understatement. It had a three-car garage, and a kitchen that would have made any cook proud. "I didn't think you could cook."

She cocked her head as though puzzled by my words. "I love cooking. It's a great stress reliever."

"That's great." I didn't want her to know that I was confusing dream Macey with real Macey. "This is a dream kitchen for sure." I knocked on the island top after circling it to admire her double stove with eight burners.

"I started cooking when I was in high school. My best friend wanted to learn how to make salsa for some school event, so we found a recipe in one of her mother's old cookbooks. It was so much fun to take a ton of ingredients and make it into something delicious. Obviously, salsa is easy, but I learned other foods," she said.

"What's your favorite thing to cook?" I asked.

"I really love baking the most. It's very delicate and requires a steady hand."

"I can't wait to taste some of your treats." I cringed at the innuendo and quickly focused my attention on the countertop and changed the topic. "This isn't granite. What is it?"

She walked over to stand opposite me. "It's soapstone."

"I like it. It gives the kitchen a warm vibe."

"This was one of the things I insisted on having when they built it," she said.

"Everything I've seen is so beautiful. When was it built?"

"Five years ago. My girlfriend at the time helped me pick out the color scheme. She's an interior designer."

My eyebrows shot up at the word "girlfriend." It was the

first real meat about her private life that she shared. "Do you still keep in touch?"

She crossed her arms, almost defensively. "Do any of us really stay in touch with our exes?"

"Touché," I said. I couldn't imagine picking up my phone and calling Christina just to check in. Besides, Tamsyn deleted her number from my phone. I could get it easily enough, but I needed to cleanse my life of her. "I couldn't imagine dealing with my ex. What happened between you, if that's not too personal?"

"She was very controlling."

I cringed. "I'm sorry. Mine accused me of working too much. She was right, but she didn't have to be so mean about it."

Macey shook her head. "They don't deserve any more of our time."

"Agreed," I said.

"Let's retire to the front room and enjoy the rest of the evening. I have a smooth whiskey that I've been saving for a special occasion."

At some point during the brief tour, Macey kicked off her shoes and let the pins out of her hair. As beautiful as her hair was up, I preferred it down and wild around her shoulders. I wanted to do the same, but it wasn't my house and I was still trying to make a good impression.

I stood by the floor-to-ceiling window that overlooked a pond with a lit-up fountain as she poured us each a glass. "This is such a peaceful view. I'd spend most of my time here." My pulse sped when she handed me a glass and our fingers touched.

"I love it, but sadly, most of my time is either spent in my study or my bedroom," she said.

We sat on the sofa with enough space between us to have a comfortable conversation, but also close enough to touch. I wasn't going to make the first move, but I was ready in case she did. "You've told me a lot about your aunt Abby and your mother, but what about the rest of your family?"

I focused on her mouth as she told me about science summer camps with her cousins, shenanigans with her best friend in high school, and how she used to be married. That got my attention.

"You were married before?" I don't know why I was so surprised. Macey was quite a catch.

"Back in medical school. Everyone told me it was a mistake, but Mickey made life and school fun. He was so exuberant. He was the kind of guy who everyone wanted to be around, you know?"

"What happened?" I wasn't even surprised that she was married to a man. I was surprised she was single.

"Drugs. He was using them to pull all-nighters to study. I didn't even see the signs until it was too late." Her hand balled into a fist. "I should've known. I should've never believed him when he said he was clean and going to NA, but I wanted to. He was my partner and I trusted him with everything."

I feared the worst. "What happened to him?"

"Last I heard, he was somewhere in California. I got a divorce and worked with his parents to get him into rehab."

"So, he never reached out to make amends?"

Her mouth flattened into a straight line. "No. I have no idea how to find him, but I've always made sure he and his parents knew they could reach out to me. Every so often I'll get an email from his parents telling me they saw I was at such and such event or they read a news story I was quoted in. I always liked them."

"It's not fair for anyone's family to have to go through something like that," I said.

Our conversation took a downward turn and I wanted to salvage it without looking like an ass, but I didn't know what to say. I had an uncle who was an alcoholic, but I didn't want to continue on this path.

"Does that fact that I was married to a man bother you?" she asked.

I shook my head. "Not at all. I take it you've dated women who had a problem with it?"

"Unfortunately, yes. I've dated a few women who thought I was experimenting with them."

I scooted closer and held her hand. "Macey, I think you're a fascinating woman. You're incredibly intelligent, you save people's lives, you're sexy, and I hope this relationship goes somewhere. I don't care that you were married. I'm sad that it ended the way it did because you didn't deserve that."

I knew she was going to kiss me because her gaze went from my eyes down to my lips several times before her mouth opened slightly and she pulled me closer.

"Thank you for firing me as your doctor," she said.

Her lips were warm and soft, but her mouth was demanding. It wasn't a gentle first kiss and I was okay with that. I knew we were going to be explosive when we finally knocked down the walls of formality. I just wasn't prepared for how fast my body reacted to hers or how well we fit in each other's arms. It was perfect. She tasted spicy and when her tongue darted across my bottom lip, I whimpered. I wrapped my hands in her hair and kept her lips against mine. This was a first kiss I was going to remember forever. The second kiss was even better. She pulled away only to push my shoulders back on the couch before she slid her dress higher on her thighs and straddled my lap. I ran my hands up and down her back and leaned forward while she pressed her body into mine.

I was expecting a nice good night kiss, but the soft, eager woman in my arms was almost too much. I wanted to flip her so her back was flat on the couch and I was grinding myself between her legs, but my elbow was still healing, so my only move was to roll my hips until we were both gasping for breath. I knew that I could come this way, but this was happening so fast, and I didn't want either of us to regret it in the morning. Her nipples were strained against the soft fabric of her dress. I wanted to pull down the front and taste her soft skin and hard nipples. Knowing I'd rip the dress if I tried, I took a gentler approach and brushed my fingertips across them instead. She bucked against my hips.

"We're going to have to stop soon," I said weakly. I opened my eyes to look at her and moved my hands down to the top of her thighs. I felt the sexual tension slowly release the hold on her body as she relaxed in my arms.

"I know. But maybe just a minute longer?"

I felt her hands on the back of my neck, and the way she bit her bottom lip, waiting for me to answer the question was a formality. We both knew I was going to say yes, but she was being polite. I simply nodded and leaned into her. She moaned when I squeezed her thighs so I moved my hands higher while she spread her legs wider. I felt the lace panties and knew we really had to stop. I dropped my hands and leaned back. My heart pulsed faster than I could count. I felt drunk with desire and need. She slowly climbed off my lap and sat in the chair opposite me. I winced when I tried straightening my dress, and she flipped into doctor mode immediately.

"Is your elbow okay? Shit, I knew I shouldn't have done that." She gingerly moved my elbow back and forth to gauge range of motion.

"Are you kidding me? That was the best thing ever." I smiled at her and touched her cheek. She was too close and too beautiful not to touch.

"I'm going to get your sling because I don't like the swelling," she said.

I saw regret in her eyes before she tried to excuse herself. I stopped her.

"Wait. Come here." I waited until she was sitting next to me. "You didn't hurt me. My elbow has been in a cast all day. It's barely swollen and it's sore because it's healing. You had nothing to do with it. Is it tender? Yes. Do I regret any of the last ten minutes? Absolutely not." I gave her a soft kiss. "I wanted this more than anything."

"I did, too. But maybe we should wait until you're completely healed before we try this again."

My mouth dropped open. "Uh, no. We can work around it

and I promise to let you know if anything we do hurts." My voice got huskier as I thought of all the things we could still do even with a healing elbow. "Also, I hate my elbow right now."

She smiled. "All of this will keep," she said.

"Promise?" I asked.

"Without a doubt," she said.

CHAPTER NINE

That's equal parts amazing and also kind of weird," Tamsyn said.

I smacked her shoulder. "You should be happy for me. I finally found somebody who isn't awful to me, who's a professional, and who's hot as fuck."

Tamsyn widened her eyes. "Language," she whispered and nodded her head in the direction of the living room where Arya was coloring.

I covered my mouth with my hand. "Sorry. Do you think she heard me?"

We were still for a few seconds. Tamsyn gave a sigh of relief. "No, but you got lucky. You know how much she likes to repeat things her Auntie Sawyer says."

"Let's back up a minute. Why do you think it's weird?" I didn't want to think about what was on her mind because deep down, it was on my mind, too.

"You had this whole fantasy experience where you dated her and now in reality, you are. But she's a totally different person," Tamsyn said. She topped off her coffee. "Have you been able to process that with your therapist?"

I shrugged. "We're just getting started. Apparently, it's going to take some serious time."

"Your mind was probably creating the perfect woman and filling in the blanks. The Macey from Junction City—"

I interrupted her. "Ladybug Junction."

"Okay, wherever. She was everything you admired in women, right? I'm no therapist, but…" She held up her hands and ended her sentence as though I was supposed to know what she meant.

"Well, this Macey is a better kisser and definitely more passionate." I was almost pouting. My best friend should be more supportive of my new relationship. Instead, she was making me question it. "Also, she knows we were dating in my dream. I told her."

"And she didn't question that?" Tamsyn blew out a deep breath. "Look, Sawyer. Maybe you should finish therapy before you get all hot and bothered over the doctor. I'm not trying to be mean, I'm trying to save you from heartache in the future. You even said you caught yourself mistaking real life Macey and dream life Macey at least twice." She held up her forefinger. "The whole outdoor stuff and mentioning that she liked camping and canoeing when in real life, she didn't like either." She held up a second finger. "And then last night you mentioned that she doesn't like cooking, but it turns out she actually does."

I needed to keep some information to myself. Then Tamsyn wouldn't be able to hold it against me. I dropped my head in my hands. "I told Macey that sometimes I mix up the worlds. She knows I'm working through things."

Tamsyn gave me a side hug on her way to the kitchen to grab a doughnut. "You know I love you and I only want what's best for you, right?"

I nodded. Tamsyn was my rock and practical voice. I was a dreamer and she was always there to ensure I didn't float away. I lowered my voice. "But don't you want me to get laid, too?"

She playfully grabbed my chin. "Of course I do, but at what expense?"

I pulled away and frowned. I was all about the "in the moment" moments in life and she wasn't. That's why she was happily married and I was making bad choice after bad choice. "She's pretty amazing, you know."

"I do know, and that's why I really want you to think about this. Talk to your therapist more. You're going twice a week, right?"

"Yes, but only because I'm bored at work and can't do a lot, so I thought I might work on my brain while my body heals." I didn't tell Tamsyn the latest about Aunt Abby because I wanted to figure it out first. And obviously the entire experience was upsetting to her. She almost lost her best friend and now I was acting unhinged and trying to push my dream into my reality instead of pulling reality from my dream. It was confusing and, truthfully, scary. "It's helping me. My therapist is working on all of me, not just what happened because of my accident." I felt shattered since my accident. I was questioning everything. Were the rest of my memories real? "This is depressing. Let's talk about something else."

She nodded. "Agreed."

I was glad she didn't press more. "I think I found a bank, and I really like the place over on Clark Street. It's right on the edge of being residential, so people won't have to drive far and there's enough space for everything I want to do." The property was one acre with a few trees, a partial fence, and enough space inside for everything I needed to offer complete pet care.

"What about the lot next to it?" Tamsyn asked.

It was an old car dealership with lots of concrete and little grass. I couldn't justify the additional cost because I didn't know what I could use the space for. I didn't need that much parking. "It's not practical."

"But it'll give you more privacy. Can you imagine if they put in a Chik-Fil-A or something hideous like that?"

It was something to think about. Veterinarian clinics were already a high stress situation for animals. Maybe some extra space was a nice sound cushion. "I can call the bank and see if they own it." I wasn't sure of the price, but Tamsyn had a valid point. Maybe I could expand and move the offices there.

"When are you thinking about talking to Oliver?"

I pinched the bridge of my nose. I could feel another headache tapping at my temple. I didn't know if I was more susceptible to headaches after the crash or because of my current situation. New outlook, new work adventure, new possible girlfriend. It was a lot to process. "After I sign the papers and there's no going back."

She handed me a bottle of Advil and a glass of water. "Here. Medicate. You can't afford to be down now."

She was right. It was Sunday and I still had some cases to review later. My elbow was throbbing, but I wasn't going to tell her that. "Good point. I should probably go home and chill for a bit. Mom's supposed to stop by later since Dad's out of town. She made onion rolls from scratch since she's bored,, and I get to be the guinea pig."

"Why don't you and your mom come over for dinner? We can grill cheeseburgers to go with those delicious onion rolls. Go home, take a nap, study some x-rays, plan surgeries, then come back with Donna and we'll have a good night."

It was a nice plan. Normally I'd jump at the chance, but I was hyper-focused on Macey and wanted to leave my night open if she was free. "I'll ask Mom what her plans are and text you later." My dad was away on a golfing trip with his buddies, and I knew Mom would love to spend time with Arya.

Tamsyn picked up her phone and quickly typed something. She smiled when she got a ding back. "No need. Your mother just texted that she's up for it and she'll pick you up at six."

She knew me too well. I would cop out and spend my night texting with Macey or waiting for a call from her. It was probably for the best. I slid from the chair, grabbed my keys, and pasted on a smile. "Need us to bring anything else?"

"Only if you want something sweet to eat. We have fruit but maybe you could pick up some cookies or brownies?"

"Will do. Thanks for the invite."

I hugged her and promised to bring delicious treats. I quickly checked my phone when I got to my car to see if I had any messages or missed calls. I wasn't about to look at my phone in front of Tamsyn. Not after everything she said. She was right, though. It was so exciting to have somebody new in my life, but it was also surreal the way it all happened.

❖

"I've missed you," Tamsyn said. She hugged my mom as though they hadn't seen each other in years when they saw each other a month ago when I got home from the hospital. Their close relationship strengthened more because of my accident. Tamsyn didn't have an understanding family, and my mom welcomed everyone, especially my queer friends.

"Thank you for the invite. I miss getting together under normal circumstances."

I threw my hands up. Well, the best I could with my cast. "It's not like I wanted to be in a coma and break my elbow and have a zillion stitches. I love our time together, too."

They snickered. It was okay to laugh about it now. And it was nice to get my mom away from the house. When she got too comfortable, it was hard to get her to go places. Right now, she still raced over every time I called.

"We know, baby." My mom pinched my cheeks and left me in the foyer with Tamsyn on her way to search out Arya. She always had a gift for her every time we all hung out. I was sure there was a shelf in the garage of nothing but kid toys that she could quickly grab on her way out to visit anyone with children.

"I don't know what we would do without Gigi," Tamsyn said.

My mom and Tamsyn came up with the nickname. They were saving "grandma" on the off chance that I would have kids. "She loves Arya so much."

"She should come over more. I think she's afraid she's

imposing. Come on. Let's find a mojito with your name on it. Since Gigi's driving, you'll be imbibing." Tamsyn laughed at her rhyme.

I followed her out to the backyard. The evening was sticky, but the backyard was partially shaded and the fans blowing over the patio helped move the heavy air away. I kicked off my shoes and dipped my feet in the pool. Somewhere in the pool house I had a bathing suit, but I wasn't in the mood to swim. This was perfectly lazy and allowed me to be a part of my family, but still alone to give me time to think about yesterday.

"Where's your girlfriend?" Arya doggy-paddled over to me and clutched the side of the pool.

I froze. Did she overhear us this morning? I stared at Tamsyn, who shrugged.

"What girlfriend?" my mom asked.

I was torn between celebrating with my mother who would, undoubtedly, jump for joy and waiting to tell her until I knew for sure there was something solid between me and Macey. One hot, passionate date did not define a relationship. I waved my mother off like it wasn't a big deal. "She's not my girlfriend. Dr. Burr and I just had dinner last night."

The cold pool water that splattered my face and chest made me yelp. "Hey. What was that for?" I shook off the excess droplets and held my shirt away from my chest. While it was refreshing, it was unexpected.

"For not telling your mother this very important news," she said.

"There's nothing to tell really. We met at the event yesterday, had a quick lunch, and I invited her to dinner because it was her birthday and she didn't have any concrete plans."

"And?"

"And what?" I asked.

"How'd it go?"

"It was good. We ate at the new restaurant in Parkview Heights. I managed to snag a last-minute reservation and we spent the evening talking about our jobs, life, and my elbow." If my mom was freaking out about my date, she was going to lose her mind when she found out I was going to quit my job, had already picked a location, and was going to start my own veterinarian clinic. She heard me talk about it before, but I don't think she realized how close I was.

"Did you kiss?" she asked.

"Yeah, did y'all kiss?" Arya giggled when I put my hands on my hips and pretended to be upset at her question. It was hard not to melt. The kid was wearing a mermaid snorkel mask that was covered in shimmering blue glitter paint.

"That's a personal question," I said.

"You and Mommy were talking about it all morning."

She rolled her eyes dramatically as though she was forced to listen to our conversation even though she was in a different room.

"You didn't have to listen." I was hoping my back and forth with Arya was cute and my mom would forget, but she was laser focused on me, and that meant I needed to spill. I looked at Tamsyn for help, but she turned to the grill to flip the burgers—but not before I saw a huge smile on her face. I wasn't getting out of this one. I made one last attempt to deflect. "Hey, aren't you a little young to hear about me kissing somebody?"

Her little shoulders lifted above the surface of the water. "Mommy and Mama kiss all the time. It's no big deal."

I pointed at her. "Wait until you're old enough to date. I'll be asking all the questions then." I couldn't believe a seven-year-old busted me in front of my mom. She giggled again. It was precious. I faced my mother.

"It was so spur of the moment that it didn't even occur to me to tell you."

"Sawyer, you could've told me on the drive over here. I mean, I've spent a lot of time with her. It's not as though it slipped your mind because you know I know her."

All eyes were on me. I caved. "I'm sorry. You're right. I

should've told you. We had a nice dinner, we kissed, and I came home." Nobody needed to know what really happened in the time between when we first kissed to when I got home. Or how it took all my willpower to untangle myself from her and leave.

"Wait. She's your doctor. Doesn't that violate some code of ethics?"

This was getting worse. "She's not my doctor anymore."

"Since when?" she asked.

"I saw her at the hospital cafeteria when I was there for a therapy appointment a while back. We started talking and she hinted that she might like to go out and so I transferred doctors." My mom was getting agitated at either what I did or that I didn't tell her this part either. "I mean, at this point, I only go in for check-ups. I have a clean bill of health." I thumped my head for effect. "And she didn't get her feelings hurt. I checked." My mom broke eye contact first and focused her attention back on Arya. "I'm sorry, Mom."

"The hot dogs are done. Cheeseburgers are about three minutes. Who wants their bun grilled?" Tamsyn asked, breaking the ramping tension.

We all piped up. I walked over to help Tamsyn while my mom helped Arya out of the pool.

"Way to go," Tamsyn said.

I handed her three buns that she placed face down on the grill. "I know. I suck. I guess I'm going to keep her in the loop from now on. And I need to tell her about my idea of quitting my job, so act surprised."

She looked at me incredulously. "You haven't told her that either?"

"I see the error of my ways. So, pretend you know nothing."

She pointed the spatula at me. "I can't guarantee what my child will share with Gigi. If we try to play like we haven't heard about this, she might rat you out. Your best bet is to have a chat with your mom on the way home. Now hand me that plate. I don't want these buns to burn."

I handed Tamsyn the plate and helped Lauren set the table. She had made potato salad and cut wedges of watermelon, honeydew, and cantaloupe. I placed the brownies in the middle of the table, out of Arya's reach. We said a quick prayer and dug in. The cheeseburgers were bigger than Mom's rolls, but they were delicious. Surprisingly, not a word more was said about Macey. Our conversation was about second grade since Arya was starting soon, teaching, missing the veterinary convention, and how Tamsyn made the best summer drinks. Macey didn't even cross my mind until I slipped into Mom's car and we pulled out of Tamsyn's driveway.

"You know I want to know more about you and Dr. Burr," she said.

"I promise to tell you from now on. There really isn't much to say now, but I do have other big news. If you're up for it."

"Nothing could shock me more than you dating your doctor."

"She's not my doctor anymore. I told you that," I said. Even though I know I did everything textbook, I still felt a little guilty. Mom's prodding didn't help.

"You know what I mean. What else is on your mind?"

I took a deep breath. "I'm going to start my own practice."

CHAPTER TEN

I was studying x-rays of one of our regular patients, Francine, a cat with a broken tail when my phone lit up with Macey's name.

"What's your week look like?"

"Hi. Well, pretty much the same as last week. Just sitting around healing," I said. I hadn't talked to her since our intense encounter Saturday night. It was Monday and I was amazed that I didn't call or text her yesterday. I caved this morning and sent her a quick "thanks for a great Saturday" text.

"I have a light schedule Wednesday and wanted to see if you wanted to maybe have dinner again or get together," Macey said.

I did a happy dance in my chair and quickly looked around to see if any of the techs saw me. "I would love that." I almost purred my answer and quickly cleared my throat. "Did you have any place in mind?"

"I can cook dinner," she said.

I knew another night at her house would put us in her bed. As much as I wanted that, I wanted a better foundation for our relationship. "Absolutely not. You're too busy, and the last thing you need to do is cook dinner. How about Donovan's? They have a lot of different options."

"Sounds good. Want me to pick you up?" she asked.

"Sure. I'll text you my address. Thank you for the invitation," I said.

She cleared her throat. "After Saturday, it's hard not to want to spend more time with you."

I froze. Did I hear her correctly? I felt lightheaded, and blood pounded in my ears. "It was hard not to text you yesterday."

Her voice grew softer and sexier. "You should have. I reviewed some cases and hung out with my family."

I smacked my forehead. "Sounds like what I did. My mom and I went over to Tamsyn's." I paused. "I'm sorry."

"Don't be sorry. We'll see each other in a few days."

I heard rustling and another voice.

"I need to go, but we'll talk soon," she said.

I didn't know how long I'd been holding my phone and staring at it until Yara nudged me.

"You have to press those funny squares to get it to work," she said.

I recovered quickly. "Ha, ha. I just got done with a call."

"Weird because you've been holding it for at least ten seconds. Oh, my God. Did you get bad news?" She put her hand on my shoulder to console me.

"No, it was very good news." I paused for effect and then dropped my good news. "I have another date."

Yara twirled me in my chair so that I faced her. "That's incredible. Who is she? They? Who is it?"

Yara was the only other queer employee. She started right after Christina dumped me, so she saw me at my lowest even though I tried hard to keep my personal life from slipping into my professional one.

"You remember the hottie from the free clinic day, right? She called to ask me out to dinner," I said. I shrugged like it was no big deal but we both knew it was massive.

"Your doctor, right?"

"Ex-doctor." I corrected her immediately. I didn't need the whole world thinking Macey was unethical.

"See? You can meet the right person in the worst circumstances. Well, I'm glad she got you to smile like that. It's good to see," she said.

"Thanks."

I tucked my phone in my pocket and studied the x-ray. The injury was near the end of Francine's tail, so she wouldn't need surgery, but her movements were going to have to be restricted. I wrote down my diagnosis and met with her owner.

"We'll reset the bones and wrap it, but you're going to have to keep her restricted to a small area while she heals. Like a bathroom or a small room in the house," I said.

Tears bubbled up in her owner's eyes. "We don't know how she got out or what happened. This is just awful." She leaned down and slipped her fingers through the carrier. "You're going to be fine, Francine. But no more sneaking out."

"I'll have one of the techs take her in the back and we'll get her fixed up. I'll also send you home with some antibiotics. Starting tomorrow, every day add a dab of ointment to the injury, replace the bandage, and keep it wrapped. Bring her back in two weeks and we'll check her out."

She blew out a hot breath. "I really wish you offered at-home services. So many people would pay for that. It's so hard to get Francine in her carrier."

That was something I would add to my list of special services once the practice was up and running. The only person doing them now was a veterinarian whose sole practice was euthanizing pets in the privacy of their homes.

"I wish we did, too," I said. I had mentioned it to Oliver when I was first hired, but he said he couldn't afford for me or another veterinarian to be away from the office that long. Time was money, and he wanted as much as he could get. I wanted to be successful, too, but having happy customers and healing pets was my number one objective no matter how long it took. I walked Francine's owner to the front desk and asked Yara to print off care instructions while they set Francine's tail.

"Call me if you have any questions or concerns."

She patted my hand. "Thank you, Dr. Noel, for always being nice and taking the time to explain things to me. You've always given Francine the best care. She loves you, and she doesn't like a lot of people."

A lot of clients requested me. Patrons like her empowered me to continue on this road. I smiled when I thought about the signs. Going to a therapist made me more aware of how people influenced my life, and I was having one of those moments right now. "Thank you for trusting me with Francine. We'll see you in two weeks."

I finished out my day shuffling papers, taking consult calls, and watching the clock. I had a six o'clock walk-through at the property I was ninety-nine percent sure I was going to buy. Tamsyn was meeting me there to either encourage me or tell me to run away. I had a feeling she was going to have me sign on the proverbial dotted line before I talked myself out of it. She was already at the property talking to the Realtor when I pulled up.

"Are you ready to make a decision?" Tamsyn asked. She opened my car door and gave me a quick hug.

"I think so. Let's see what my future can look like," I said.

Our Realtor Patty reviewed specifications including inside square footage, outside space, and average utilities costs, then disappeared while Tamsyn and I put our heads together.

"I love it. I think this is exactly what you need." She handed me her tablet where she had roughly designed the area based on previous conversations. "You'll have four examination rooms here. And you and at least three staff members can have offices." She pointed to the east side of the building. "You can extend this for the grooming area and add a small hallway here to go to the kennels and backyard. That shouldn't cost a lot."

It made sense. Tamsyn's brother-in-law was a contractor and gave me a ballpark price on how much construction would cost and how long it would take. I padded his numbers into my business proposal. I did a slow walk around the place, keenly aware that both the Realtor and Tamsyn were watching my every step. It was a risk. I was borrowing a lot of money during a time when interest rates were high and there was no guarantee I would succeed. But my recent coma taught me nothing was a guarantee.

"Let's do it," I said.

Tamsyn's shout echoed in the empty space. I plugged my ears dramatically until she raced over and pulled me into a bear hug.

"This is so wonderful. I know there's a lot to do, but I'm going to help you every step of the way," Tamsyn said. She was in the thick of everything when her parents opened their nursery, Flower Power. She knew how to file for the correct licenses, what paperwork needed to be filled out, and how to work with the contractors. Since her brother-in-law had a construction company, she promised they would be cheap and efficient.

I shrugged. "What now?"

Patty stepped over to us. "As soon as you settle on a bank, we'll extend an offer and then we go for it."

I was already pre-approved at Southern Bank of America. "We're not going to offer them asking price, right? I mean, this place has been vacant for six months, and it's going to need a new roof, new plumbing, and more work than even we expected."

Patty shook her head. "Never offer full asking price for those very reasons. There's a lot of work that has to be done. They know it and so do we." She pointed to her tablet. "The owners are from Arkansas, so they'll be happy to unload it."

"I guess extend a lowball offer and see if it sticks," I said. The moment I'd been waiting for since I graduated veterinary school was finally happening. Shit. I needed to show my parents. "Can we hang around here for a bit? I want to show my mother the place. I've left her out of a lot of decisions recently, and I feel she'll disinherit me if she doesn't see this before I sign."

"You can lock up whenever you're ready. Here's the key. Just put it in the lock box when you're done and don't forget to padlock the gate," Patty said.

"Thank you, Patty." I pulled out my phone and dialed my mom.

"Hey, what are you and Dad doing tonight?"

"Nothing. Just watching *Wheel of Fortune*. What's going on?"

"I wanted to know if you could meet me at 202 Clark Street."

"Right now?"

I knew getting her out would be difficult. "It's a surprise, Mom. Put your shoes on, shake Dad awake. I'm going to send you a pin. Just follow the directions. It should only take you about ten minutes."

"Okay, honey. Give us time to get ready. We'll be there in a bit."

I found Tamsyn in the back office, hands on her hips, staring out the window.

"The parents will be here soon," I said.

She turned. "Huzzah! You need to share this with them. They are going to be so proud. Also, I decided this has to be your office. It's so peaceful. And if you want, you can knock down that wall and make it even bigger."

The twelve-by-twelve area was small, but I didn't want to take away square footage from the exam rooms or surgery ward or even the reception area. "This is fine. It frees up space for more important things."

I walked back to the front and waited for the familiar silver sedan with worn paint on the roof to pull into the parking lot. My mom refused to let my dad waste money on a paint job and my dad refused to buy a new car. Their ten-year-old Toyota with over 100,000 miles was their stalemate. I found a small piece of copper wire and wrapped it and unwrapped it around my finger while I anxiously waited for them to pull up. I was super nervous. What if they hated the idea? What if they pointed out how stupid it was to borrow so much money on the cusp of a recession?

"Quit fidgeting. You already lost your elbow for six weeks. Don't lose a finger, too," Tamsyn said.

I handed her the wire and flexed my finger to get the blood flowing again. "What's taking them so long?"

She looked at her watch. "It's only been eight minutes. Let's walk around the back and figure out where the kennels will be and where the playdate area will go."

"I really love that idea. And that might even help with the animals' anxiety of going to the vet." The more time I spent here, the deeper I fell in love with the place. Unfortunately, the crew would have to clear out some of the brush and trees for more outdoor space. I wanted to keep as many trees as possible, though, for shade and for giving it a realistic outdoor vibe. Too many veterinary clinics had small grassy areas, but they weren't big enough or natural enough.

Before I had a chance to banter with her, I heard the crunch of tires hitting gravel and looked to the parking lot to see my parents' car pulling into a spot near the front of the building. "Let's go."

"What's going on here, honey?" My mom climbed out of the car and stared at the blue and white building.

I hugged her and looked at what she was seeing as though I, too, was seeing it for the first time. The graffiti was bold and invasive, and the porcelain letters that once spelled out the name of a denture and implant business were smashed and faded.

"Mom. Dad. I've mentioned in the past that I was seriously considering starting my own practice." I pointed to the building. "I want to convert this to a clinic. Well, not just a clinic. Something bigger with more services than we have at Oliver's practice now."

"Did you quit your job?" Dad asked. He was clearly surprised. Apparently, Mom didn't tell him my plan.

"Not yet, but I'm going to. I'm probably going to sign paperwork this week and tell Oliver I'm quitting once we start rolling on this. Remember the crew who redesigned your kitchen?"

"Oh, I love my kitchen. It's so beautiful. Tamsyn's family, right?" Mom asked. She was still processing everything now that it was more than just empty words when I drove her home the other night.

Dad pulled me into his arms. "I think it's great, pumpkin. You do what you want to do. If this makes you happy, then go for it."

Mom was a harder sell. I pushed. "Let's go inside and I'll show you what I'm envisioning."

"When is this all going to happen, Sawyer Marie?" It was never good when she used my middle name. That meant I had some explaining to do even though I thought I explained it in the car.

"Well, I can get started if the sellers accept my offer and I sign the business loan. Jeremy always has a crew ready to do some work. I think that by the end of fall I can open the doors."

That timeframe was probably wishful thinking. The architect redesign would take at least three weeks and the reconstruction two months after that. I was quiet while my mom toured the building with Tamsyn. I rolled on the balls of my feet while I waited.

"Don't worry about your mother. You know she'll support you. She just fights change. I bet you she'll be up here all the time. It's so close to the house." Dad opened his arms to me.

I walked into his hug. "I hope you're right."

"She'll probably come by during construction and want to help or offer the crew sandwiches and cookies. You might as well make her the honorary foreman now."

When my mother returned to the reception area, I couldn't tell what she was feeling. I didn't know if she approved or not until Tamsyn gave me a discreet thumbs-up. I bit back a smile. "Mom, let me show you outside and what we're planning to do there."

Tamsyn handed me her tablet with a bird's eye view of the yard and woods. I pointed to where we were standing so my mom had her bearings. "So over here we'll have an open space for the dogs to run and play if they're boarded. The runs will go here, and I want to put a playdate area over here."

"What does that mean?" she asked.

"Just an area for our clients to hang out and let their pets play."

"They'll have to be up-to-date on their rabies shots and all vaccines, right?" she asked.

I nodded. "Definitely. And it's off to the side and back so that patients coming into the facility won't be distracted by them," I said.

"You'll have to do it by sign-up or people will stay forever," Tamsyn said.

Princess's owner immediately popped in my head. "For sure. Maximum play time will be one hour. And if they want more time, they'll have to pay. Unless somebody else is on the schedule." I smiled when I realized all our attention was focused on the wrong thing. I directed the conversation back to why I was going out on my own. "I've always wanted my own practice. I don't like how Oliver marches people in and out as fast as possible."

"But he's rich and has a nice car," my mother said.

"I drive a nice car."

We all walked away from that comment.

"I think it's great and I'm pretty sure you could find something to do here, Donna, if you wanted to," Tamsyn said.

I looped my arm through Mom's. "What do you think?"

She kissed my forehead and squeezed my arm. "I'm so proud of you. Just tell me when and where you need me and I'll be here."

I swallowed the lump in my throat and clapped my hands. "Then welcome to Healing Paws."

CHAPTER ELEVEN

Our date took a melancholy turn when Macey told me she'd lost a patient that day. I did my best to keep our subject matter light. It was a nice night for a walk. A quick storm had blown away the stiff oppressive heat that blanketed our days. We had a late dinner at Donovan's and decided to take a stroll in the park across the street. She slid her hand in mine as we talked about everything but our jobs. Losing a patient was hard even if you knew the chances of recovery were slim. I felt the tension in her grip and saw how the weight of her day pulled the corners of her mouth down.

"Today I treated an overweight guinea pig named Crackers because guess what? He loves crackers," I said. She smiled a bit. I continued telling stories until I got a real smile out of her. "We treated a parrot who kept yelling profanities. You could still hear him with the door closed. The funny thing about that is that many of the patrons who were in the waiting room had no idea and thought we had a very irate client in one of the rooms."

"What kind of things was he saying?" she asked. Her grip on my hand lessened.

"My favorite was when he said 'shut your pie hole' repeatedly. His owners were beyond embarrassed. According to them, they watch a lot of television and some phrases stick."

"Why was he there? What's was wrong with him?" she asked.

"He has allergies, so we treat him several times a year. They must have binged *The Sopranos* or something recently. The f-bombs and other expressions he squawked sounded mobster-like." If she only knew how her soft laugh, even brushed with sadness, made my stomach flip. "I have an idea. Why don't we go to the carnival and try to win some overpriced stuffed animals or ride the Ferris wheel?"

She looked at me as if I had suggested we rob the place. "I don't like carnivals or rides," she said.

We were walking toward the one camped out at the other side of the park. The flashing bright lights filled the horizon, and I couldn't help but smile at the distant shouts of thrill seekers. "I thought you liked them," I said.

She stopped and blew out a deep breath. "No, my aunt Abby fell out of a roller coaster, so now they scare me. We've never had a conversation about carnivals before. You know I'm not the same woman who was in your dreams, right? Maybe you dreamt about us having that conversation, but we did not." She motioned her forefinger almost angrily between us. I heard the annoyance in her clipped voice.

I had done it again. I mixed my worlds. "You're right. I'm sorry. Is there anything you'd like to do tonight?"

She stopped walking. "It's getting late and I'm sorry, but I'm horrible company. Can we do this some other time? I just have a lot on my mind and I should've taken you up on your offer to reschedule."

"I'm glad I got to see you. I'm just sorry it was a bad day," I said. I didn't feel good about the direction of the date, but I was trying. We walked back in silence. She apologized again before she slipped into her car and drove away. What just happened?

"Aren't you supposed to be on a date?" Tamsyn answered her phone on the second ring.

"Are you asleep? I'm sorry." I'd been apologizing too much tonight. "And yeah, but we ended it early. She lost a patient today."

"Well, that's awful. What happened?"

I waited for my Bluetooth to kick in. "She didn't want to talk about it, so I talked about a few patients I saw. Remember Jimmy the parrot?"

"Oh, my God. Don't even tell me he died," Tamsyn said.

"No, he came in cursing like a sailor and had us all in stitches. Hard to be professional when he's screaming 'fuck off' and 'don't touch me' over and over and while Meredith was treating him."

Her laugh was robust and genuine. "I love it. I can only imagine what goody two-shoes Meredith thought."

"She was sweating profusely but managed to give him his treatment. This is exactly why home visits are going to be popular, I think."

"Oh, totally. Charge a travel fee of like fifteen bucks and we'll get you hooked up with Square so you or whoever can collect payments out in the field. No open accounts until you're established," she said.

"Yes, boss."

"So, that can't be the only reason you called. What else happened?"

I dreaded fessing up, but I needed her to tell me it was going to be okay. "I mixed my worlds again. And tonight wasn't the night for that."

I told her the story, hoping it wasn't as bad as I thought. Judging by the intake of breath over the phone, I knew I fucked up.

"Oh, that's bad. You really need to find that line."

"All I wanted was to make her smile. And who doesn't love carnivals? The smells, the flashing lights, the spinning rides, and the funnel cakes." I distinctly remember talking about fairs and carnivals, but the more I thought about it, the more I recalled the conversation happened with a very different Macey. I expected a scolding, but Tamsyn obviously felt sorry for me.

"Quit beating yourself up. It's bad, but it's not the end of the world. It's not like you called her by a different name in the throes of passion. And she knows your history, so she's just having a bad day."

A beep interrupted our conversation. I glanced at the screen on my dashboard. "Oh, shit. She's calling me. I'll call you back." I disconnected the call before Tamsyn had a chance to say bye. "Hello?"

"Hi."

Macey's smooth voice filled my speakers. Instantly, I thought something bad happened. "Are you okay?"

"I'm home and fine. I wanted to apologize for tonight," she said.

My shoulders relaxed and I loosened my grip on the steering wheel. "That's good to hear." I didn't want to push, so I waited for her to speak.

"Are you home yet?" she asked.

"About five minutes out. Did you need something?"

"I know it's late and I ran away about fifteen minutes ago, but can you come over?"

The rumble strips startled me back to reality and I straightened the tires back on the road. "Um, sure. Do you need anything?"

"Just you."

Those words melted me. "I'll be there in ten." I drove faster than the speed limit knowing she needed me. This was the moment I wanted. I checked my face in the rearview mirror before pulling up to the gate. I punched in the code and parked in her driveway. She greeted me at the door wearing silky lounge pants and an oversized cashmere top. Her hair was pulled back with a simple black tie. A glass of wine dangled from her fingertips.

"Thanks for coming over." She stepped back so I could enter. "Can I get you a nightcap?"

I sat on her sofa. "Since it's late, I'd love a glass of water." It was ten thirty and I told myself I would leave in an hour no matter what. She had to be at work at eight, and after a day like today, I was surprised she wasn't curled up in a little ball on her bed.

"I wasn't fair to you tonight," she said.

I squeezed her hand to show support and smiled when she interlocked our fingers. "It's okay. Sometimes I struggle with reality, and I'm working on figuring it out still."

She sat up and looked into my eyes. "Are you having any issues? Confusion? Double vision?"

I touched her cheek to ease her concern. "No. I'm fine. I have no symptoms. I jog on the treadmill and do mind exercises like you prescribed. I even watch *Jeopardy*. The reality versus dream is something I'm working on." There was a lot of nervous energy radiating off her. I dropped my hand and sat back. "Do you want to talk about today? Or about anything? Hell, we can even pull up old episodes of *Jeopardy* or I can find a trivia game to get your mind off today."

Her answer was pulling me close to her and kissing me soundly. She felt soft in my arms, but I felt desperation on her lips. "I needed this. You. To feel alive after such a shitty day."

We had agreed to take things slow and get to know each other better, so I wasn't sure if this was a test. I pulled her in my arms and held her. She rested her head on my shoulder. That was the right thing to do. Eventually, I felt her pulse retreat to normalcy and the energy shift into something calmer.

"What is your favorite holiday?" I asked. I felt the shake of her body against mine as she giggled.

"That's random," she said.

I was extremely aware of her hand on my thigh. Her body language screamed that she wanted more than my arms around her, but I didn't want to screw this up by jumping into bed with her. I totally understood the need to feel alive after what happened, but I figured talking and holding her would work, too.

"You know, a favorite holiday says so much about somebody. For example, my favorite holiday is Christmas. Not because of the presents, but because of family. Me, Tamsyn, Lauren, and Arya go to my parents' house and eat a big meal, watch holiday movies, and exchange gifts. It's the most relaxed we are all year.

We don't think about our jobs or patients. We celebrate each other and play games and sing songs. It's a real Hallmark movie come to life."

"That sounds wonderful. Since I have a lot of family, Christmas is a big deal, too, but I like Easter. The weather is warm, we're outside hiding or finding eggs, and we're all there. Christmas is hard because everyone splits their time between different houses, so we're never all at the same place."

"Just how big is your family?" I asked.

"Let's see. My parents, three brothers, four nephews, two nieces, two aunts, one uncle, one great-uncle, six cousins, and my grandmother. So, quite a few. And sometimes in-laws will show up, too. Large families can be overwhelming, but I'm happy I have such a large support group."

"Are your brothers as successful as you?"

"One's a lawyer, one owns a camping supplies store, and the other one is an accountant," she said.

"It sounds like your entire family is successful. Your parents must be so proud. Especially of you. You found your career because of your aunt. How many people can say their daughter is a brain surgeon?" I finally got a full, hearty laugh out of her.

"I'm not a brain surgeon. I'm a neurologist," she said.

I knew the difference, but she needed some lighthearted fun, so I played dumb. "So, you don't perform lobotomies or cut into skulls and zap the brain with electrical prods?"

She shook her head. "No, only nonsurgical methods to help people. It works most of the time."

Fuck. I made the mistake of bringing up her job. My mind screamed "abort" and tried to think of anything besides work. "I also like Valentine's Day because I'm a romantic at heart." That wasn't any better. This was technically our second date. "And who doesn't like beer for St. Patrick's Day?"

"I'm not a beer drinker," she said.

"How do you feel about Halloween?" I asked.

"It's okay. We don't get a lot of trick-or-treaters. I usually go over to my parents' house if I'm not still at work."

"Are your nieces and nephews still into trick-or-treating?" I leaned forward so I could look her in the eyes. "I still don't know how old you are." A ripple of heat surged through my body at her smile. It was sexy and flirty. I shrugged. "I really don't know."

"How old do you think I am?"

I dropped my head back on the couch and closed my eyes. I walked into that one. "Let's see. Undergrad, medical school, residency." I opened an eye and peered at her. "You graduated high school at eighteen, right?" At her nod, I closed my eye again and did the math. "Looking at you, I would say you're twenty-nine or thirty, but based on your education and how established you are, I'm going to go with thirty-five?"

"Is that a question?"

"Am I right?" I studied her face and shook my head. "You don't have any wrinkles."

Her eyes darted over my face and landed on my lips. "You're thirty-four."

I scoffed. "I was your patient, so you knew my age months ago."

She touched my face and ran her finger over one cheek, across my forehead and back down the other cheek. "You look incredible."

Heat spread from within and splashed on my cheeks. I looked away for a moment to hide my embarrassment. I wasn't used to compliments. Macey was out of my league, but that didn't stop me from trying. Getting a new shot at life changed a person. I was a little more confident than I was before, and I stopped caring so much about what everybody thought. "Thank you. But also, you still haven't told me your age."

She looked at me smugly. "I like keeping you guessing."

I tilted my head and gave her a look.

She threw up her hands in defeat. "Okay, I'm thirty-seven."

"You look incredible," I said.

Her eyes looked green in the soft glow of the lamp. They darted from my eyes, down to my mouth, and back up. She wanted to kiss me but knew that if we started, it would be hard to stop. My phone dinged with a text message, breaking the moment and startling both of us.

"Is everything okay?" Macey asked.

I smiled and nodded. "I forgot to send Tamsyn a message."

Are you okay? You never called me back. I see you're at her house. She didn't murder you, did she?

I'm sorry! All is well. Just hanging out.

"Sorry about that. We were on the phone when you called me," I said.

"I didn't mean to interrupt you. Do you need to call her?" she asked.

It was almost midnight. I broke my own promise of leaving at eleven thirty. "No. Everything is fine."

"She really cares about you."

"She's my ride or die."

My body was humming as Macey curled against me. I encircled her and held her. I played with her hair and told her stories about my youth. When her questions stopped and her breathing evened out, I realized she was finally asleep. I gently laid her head down on the couch and slipped into the small space behind her. The last thing I remember was feeling her arm reach back and hold me close to her.

Chapter Twelve

O liver, can we schedule a meeting soon?" I leaned against the doorframe of his office as though my heart wasn't pounding furiously in my chest and my hands weren't sweating profusely.

"Of course." He pulled out his weekly planner and skimmed its contents. "I'm out most of next week, but how about next Friday at four thirty?"

It was better than I hoped. I secured the loan, purchased the property, and had a fast closing date only two weeks away. I planned on giving Oliver three weeks' notice because I felt guilty. I knew anybody they hired to replace me was going to need training. "That sounds great."

He pointed at my elbow. "How are you doing? Is it all healed?"

A part of me wondered if he was concerned or just tired of pulling his weight. It had been a long time since he was in the office this much seeing patients. "It's just about as good as new. Therapy has worked its magic." I moved my elbow back and forth several times without wincing to prove my point.

"That's great. When is your last therapy session?"

Okay, so it was about work. "Next Thursday. I should get a clean bill of health at the end of the week." I didn't tell him I was going to a different kind of therapy. That was none of his business and didn't affect my job.

"Great."

I left his office and grabbed my messenger bag before leaving for the evening. I hadn't seen Macey since I woke up on her couch last week. She threw herself into work and our communication consisted of phone tag and several text messages. She was busy during the days with work, and I was busy after hours signing papers, meeting with contractors, and waiting until the place was mine. I didn't have the keys yet, but Patty didn't think there would be a problem. The owners wanted a quick sale and I was itching to get started on my new life.

My phone lit up with a call from Tamsyn. I answered and was surprised to hear Arya's voice. "Come over for a swim, Auntie Sawyer."

My stress immediately vanished. "How am I supposed to say no to you?"

"I don't know. That's why Mom made me call you."

"Ask your mom what's for dinner."

She yelled at Tamsyn, who yelled back from another room. I winced and held the phone away from my ear. I heard every word Tamsyn said and every word Arya repeated.

"Okay, I'll be there in thirty minutes." I wanted to change my clothes.

"Mom says to invite your new girlfriend, too," Arya said.

I was pleasantly surprised that Tamsyn invited Macey and equally excited to extend the invitation. "Tell her I will. See you later, peanut."

I hung up and checked the time. Macey was done with rounds, but probably still at the hospital. I shot her a text.

Tamsyn invited us to dinner and a swim but the swim is optional. That's more Arya. I wasn't sure if you were busy tonight or not. I hit send before I overthought it. Three dots popped up immediately and my entire focus was on my phone. Waiting took forever. I had to reread her words several times before they sank in.

I need a break. Dinner with your friends sounds lovely. I

*need to finish some paperwork, but I can meet you there if you
give me their address.*

Great. I'll see you later.

I needed to find the perfect outfit that wasn't too casual but
not over-the-top runway ready. I settled on a sleeveless V-neck
blouse, a pair of shorts, and strappy sandals. Normally, I'd throw
on an athletic T-shirt and a pair of jogging shorts and throw my
hair back in a ponytail, but tonight I was trying harder.

She'll be there.

I wasn't planning on swimming, but I grabbed a suit that
was more flattering than the ones I had stashed at Tamsyn's. I
freshened my makeup, brushed my hair, and bolted. Tamsyn was
going to have to calm me down. I was at her house in fifteen
minutes.

"She's coming," I said.

"She's coming," Tamsyn echoed. She grabbed my hand and
pulled me to a chair. "I didn't think she'd actually accept the
invitation, but I'm happy she did. Lauren's doing a quick sweep
of the house for anything embarrassing lying around."

"I didn't think she'd say yes either. She's been pushing
herself at work and I haven't seen her since last week," I said.

"The sleepover," Tamsyn said.

"The benign sleepover," I said.

Tamsyn rolled her eyes. "That's such a horrible word to use
when you're talking about heart stuff."

"The chaste sleepover? The PG sleepover?" I suggested.

"How about the time you fell asleep in each other's arms?"
she asked.

I stood and paced in front of her. "You're giving me mixed
signals. Do I go for it or not? I mean, you tell me to back off, but
then invite her over."

Tamsyn grabbed my hands. "Calm down. You're an adult.
I'm merely trying to help you not blow it with somebody
fantastic."

"I know. I'm sorry for being all over the place. And you're

right. Let's have a good night. Now put me to work so I'm not thinking about her and looking at the door." I took the Coke from her outstretched hand.

"Why don't you watch Arya? She wants to swim, but she can't go in the water unless somebody's with her. I'll finish up dinner and I'll let you know when Macey's here," Tamsyn said.

She shooed me to the backyard where Arya was swinging on the playset.

"Auntie Sawyer! You're here. Let's go swimming." She jumped out of her swing and tore off her T-shirt and shorts. She stood at the side of the pool in her bathing suit and dived into the pool at my nod. It was a good ten seconds before she surfaced. Even though she was only seven years old, she had been swimming since before she could walk. "Aren't you coming in?"

I sat on the edge of the pool with my legs in the water. Had Macey said she wasn't coming by, I would have been in the water with Arya, but I wanted to stay clean, fresh, and dressed. Even though Macey had her hands on my curves during our makeout session, she hadn't seen me scantily clad. I was nervous to be in a swimsuit in front of somebody who got my heart racing.

"Maybe after dinner. My friend is coming by and I don't want to get wet until she gets here," I said.

"Your girlfriend, you mean?" Arya asked. She sang the question in a teasing way. When did she grow up?

"Sort of. But don't you say anything or I will dunk you!"

She squawked and bobbed over to the other side of the pool before chanting, "Auntie's got a girlfriend. Auntie's got a girlfriend."

I riffled through the pool accessories storage box and found exactly what I was looking for—a large water gun. She squealed when she saw it and turned her back to me.

"What's the matter, Arya?" I dipped the tip of the gun into the water to load.

"Are you seriously going to drown my daughter?" Tamsyn yelled somewhere behind me, but I kept my eye on Arya.

"She's teasing me," I said. I growled through gritted teeth and hunched over like a deranged monster. I dragged my left leg behind me for a full zombie effect and clutched the water gun to my chest. I inched my way slowly over to her while she swam along the side several steps ahead of me but still within soaking distance. I gave a little roar and she responded with a gleeful shout. It was the sound of a child who was having a great time, and it was impossible to hide my smile. It wasn't until I got to the other side that I saw Lauren, Tamsyn, and Macey watching me. It was a good thing I was so far away because I felt instant heat to my face, chest, and neck. I was more than embarrassed. I was mortified. I stood and lowered the gun to my side.

Tamsyn shook her head. "It's too late. We all saw you."

"Hi, Miss Macey from the hospital," Arya said.

Macey walked over to Arya and squatted. "It's good to see you again." She pointed to me. "Want me to have a talk with her?" Arya nodded. Macey walked over with playful determination, and something hidden behind her back. I'd never seen her so casual. Shorts, a T-shirt, and flip-flops. They were nice leather ones, but still, the casual look was incredibly appealing. "So, you're picking on a baby now?"

"She's hardly a baby. She's seven. She can read, write, and swim like a fish. I'm trying to teach her not to be a bully. We don't want to raise a bully in this house."

Macey tilted her head and nodded slowly. "So, a giant water gun versus a child in a pool. Don't you think that's entirely too easy? Like shooting fish in a barrel?" She turned to the others. "Is that fair?"

"Noooo," Lauren and Tamsyn said in unison. Arya giggled and splashed closer to her parents.

Macey reached out. "Give me the water gun."

"I don't care how cute you look or how you've managed to wrap the entire family around your little finger in like five minutes, you're not getting this." I tossed it in the water and smirked victoriously. It was far enough away from everyone, and

I knew Arya wasn't going to be able to reach it without a lot of effort.

"Well, that was a mistake," Macey said.

I laughed. "She's not allowed on this side of the line."

"But I am."

"You're not going to jump in. Look, it's too far to reach it." I pointed to the water gun that was lazily floating at least three feet from any edge.

"No, but I have this." Macey pulled a smaller water gun from behind her back. I yelped at the first shot and ran around the pool with Macey hot on my heels, feeling shot after shot into my back and legs.

"No running in the pool area," Tamsyn said.

We instantly fell into a very fast walk. I made it to the safety of the house and burst inside. Macey handed Tamsyn the gun and followed me.

"You made it," I said breathlessly.

Macey walked over to me, put her hands on my waist, and kissed me hello. "I made it."

"I've missed you," I said. Every part of my body felt light. Like my heart was skipping and my feet were barely touching the ground. I liked feeling this way.

"Here I am." She slid her hands into the back pockets of her shorts. I looked her up and down and liked what I saw.

"I don't think I've ever seen you this relaxed." She reminded me of dream Macey.

"I needed a relaxing night out."

"And chasing me with a water gun is relaxing?"

She shrugged and moved closer. "I couldn't have you picking on a sweet little girl."

I pulled her against me. "You say that now. Wait until you get to know her." I brushed my lips across hers again. She slipped her hands behind my neck and deepened the kiss. It was smooth and demanding and I put my hands on her hips to steady my weak knees. In the distance, I heard someone clear their throat and eventually tore myself away from Macey's warm, full lips.

"Dinner's ready and the monster knows to leave all pool play at the pool. She won't shoot you until after dinner," Tamsyn said. She gave me a thumbs-up before Macey turned around.

"Thanks. We'll be out there in a minute." I didn't want to stop kissing Macey, but now wasn't the time. "Thank you for coming," I said to Macey.

"Thank you for the invitation." She locked our fingers together. "Now let's eat. I'm hungry. I skipped lunch."

"Sit next to me." Arya pointed to the empty chair next to her. She patted the cushion. "It's dry."

"Me?" I asked.

She shook her head and pointed at Macey.

Tamsyn chimed in. "You need to ask Macey nicely. We don't grunt and point in this house."

"Miss Macey, will you please sit next to me?"

At first, I was disappointed we weren't going to sit next to each other, but then I realized it was easier to keep eye contact from across the table. I sat next to Tamsyn. We said grace and filled our plates.

"Peanut, less talking, more eating," Tamsyn said. Arya stabbed a shrimp and popped it in her mouth. Tamsyn nodded her approval.

"This is delicious. Thank you again for inviting me. I don't get a lot of home-cooked meals during the week," Macey said.

"We're so happy you agreed. Both Lauren and I love to cook," Tamsyn said.

I didn't know what to talk about, but Lauren was so smooth at keeping a conversation going. "I had two years of culinary school, so I learned a lot of the basics," she said.

"That's incredible. Are you a chef?" Macey asked.

"Not professionally, but I'm not bad. I did it as a hobby because I love food and learning different ways to prepare it. In my family, we hung out in the kitchen and learned from Mamaw. Are you from Louisiana?" Lauren asked.

Macey nodded and took a sip of wine. "My entire family lives about twenty minutes from me."

"That's so wonderful," Lauren said.

"Do you have any hobbies?" Tamsyn asked.

"I know this sounds like I don't have a life, but I work a lot. I do crossword puzzles for downtime and watch really bad game shows."

"Like *The Price Is Right* and *Let's Make A Deal*?" Lauren asked.

Macey nodded. "And trivia shows."

"Like *Jeopardy* and *Who Wants to Be a Millionaire*," I said. Those were the shows she recommended to me.

"Anything that stimulates the brain," she said. "Even exercise. There are tons of different things."

Tamsyn looked at me. "That explains your nights on the treadmill."

"I can't afford to lose any brain function." As soon as I said it, I regretted it. Even though I hadn't met her, Macey's aunt popped in my head. I looked at Macey to see if my insensitive words upset her, but she didn't seem fazed by it. "I mean, nobody does. I'll do whatever it takes to stay sharp."

"How bad was Sawyer when she was in her wreck?" Lauren asked.

"Is this appropriate table talk?" I asked, discreetly thumbing in Arya's direction.

"It's reality. Arya knows you hurt your head and that you're fine now," Tamsyn said.

"We weren't sure. It was obvious she hit her head even though her airbag went off. She probably did it when she rolled the car." Macey looked at Arya to see how she was processing the information and continued. "Once we believed her brain was functioning normally, we tapered off the medication and she gradually regained consciousness. She responded well after she woke up. She knew her name and the date. She knew all of you and who her parents were. It was a really good sign five minutes after she woke up that her injuries were more physical than cerebral."

"Isn't eight days in an induced coma a long time, though? I always thought they only did it for a few days," Lauren said.

"It's always on a case-by-case basis, and also she didn't want to wake up," Macey said.

I gave Tamsyn a look because I didn't want her to point out the reason why.

"That's so interesting. You must learn so much at your job," Tamsyn said.

"The more I learn, the less I know," Macey said.

"Do you have a cat?" Arya asked Macey.

I laughed. "Where did that question come from?"

"I was bored. I don't understand what you're talking about. Do you have a cat?" Arya repeated.

"No, sadly, I don't have any pets. I work a lot and it wouldn't be fair to my pet if I was gone all the time," Macey said. She looked around the patio. "Do you have any pets? I haven't seen any."

"I have a hamster. Do you want to see him?" Arya jumped up from the table ready to run to her room. She was brimming with excitement to show off her fluffy friend.

"Absolutely not during dinner. Park it on your chair and maybe after we're all done you can show Miss Macey your hamster," Tamsyn said.

Arya's face fell at the news that she had to stay seated until we were all done. It broke my heart, so I finished my plate quickly and pushed it away. "That was delicious. Thank you."

Macey followed suit. "Yes. I really appreciate it."

Tamsyn looked between us. "Okay, fine. Arya, show Macey Harry the hamster."

It was precious how Arya held Macey's hand and led her inside. Once the sliding door shut, Tamsyn and Lauren leaned across the table to whisper about Macey.

"She's gorgeous. I mean, she was attractive in the hospital, but I never studied her face or her mannerisms. She's playful, loves kids, smart as fuck, and likes you. She's the whole package. So, what's wrong with her?" Lauren asked.

I beamed with pride. Macey was quite the catch. "She's a workaholic. She doesn't have a lot of downtime. That's been a problem in her past relationships."

"Well, it looks like she found her match in you. You work long hours and now you'll be even busier as you dive into your own business," Tamsyn said.

I know she meant it one way, but I took it a different, darker way. With all our time invested in our jobs, would we have time for each other? Like I wasn't already stressed with trying to work out the two Maceys in my head, but could I give her my heart if we only saw each other a few times a month?

CHAPTER THIRTEEN

Macey slid into the passenger side of my car. "How'd it go with Oliver?"

It was Friday night and I was still stressed over the conversation. I was going to lie and tell her everything was okay, but he was a total ass about my resignation. He pointed out every favor he did for me as though he had a mental running tally. I rolled my eyes and reminded him that I helped him, too. Once he realized I was serious, he backed down and thanked me for wanting to stay and help train the new hires he had to bring in-house.

"Let's just say I'm glad it's my weekend off and I don't have to think of that place until Monday," I said.

She ran her hand down my arm. "I'm sorry it was bad. Your boss sounds like a real tool."

"He really is. I'm glad I'm getting out of there. It's scary, but hopefully rewarding. Now I get to do what I want to do."

"I'm proud of you," Macey said.

Her words brought me back into the moment. I crushed my bitterness toward Oliver and his practice and tucked them away. He didn't deserve to occupy my mind on such a special occasion. We were going to see *Hamilton*. I'd seen it twice, but it was Macey's first time. "Thank you. I'm excited and a bit overwhelmed at everything."

"I'm sure starting your own practice is stressful, but it's

going to be wonderful. Everything about your business plan is a success. Especially the playdate area. I can't tell you how fun that sounds," Macey said.

I had the best support system in the world. My friends, my family, and my possible girlfriend were all one hundred percent behind me. "I can't wait for the contractors to get started. Jeremy has five guys waiting for the keys. They'll have it done in no time." I glanced over at Macey and realized I was being self-absorbed. She looked amazing. Her hair was styled up, and her red dress had a long slit down the side that showed a lot of leg. I blocked out everything else but her. "You look beautiful tonight. I'm glad we're doing this."

"I haven't been to a play in forever. Sometimes it's nice to dress up without having to attend fundraisers and talk about my job or beg for money," she said.

I wanted to kiss her, but I didn't want to smear her perfectly applied lipstick. Her pouty, plump lips were the first thing I noticed about her every time I saw her. Amplified by the same red color lipstick as her dress, it was impossible to look away from them.

"You're staring," she said.

"You're beautiful." A pink blush spread across her cheeks and she turned to look out the window. "I'm serious. I'm so happy you're my date this evening," I said.

"Thank you. It appears we have a lot to celebrate tonight. You, me, us," she said.

"I like the way that sounds. Us." I didn't know where my confidence was coming from, but I wanted her to know that I was committed without scaring the shit out of her. Tonight felt like a turning point, and I had high hopes for another night at her place that didn't involve falling asleep on the couch and waking up with a crick in my neck.

Macey held my hand on the way into the theater. I didn't know anybody there, but she did and stopped several times to say hello and introduce me to colleagues and family friends. She didn't drop my hand or shy away from letting people know we were there together. She was charming and engaging and I was floating.

"Dr. Macey Burr. How are you?"

Macey took two full steps backward after she turned to see who called her name. I immediately knew this was not somebody she was okay with having in her personal space. A woman with long, black flowing hair gave Macey a full up and down before dropping a smile that hinted at intimacy. I felt the tension in Macey even though her face and body language showed no outward signs of distress. I smiled at the woman to be polite and stared into stunning light blue eyes framed by an oval-shaped face and creamy skin. She was beautiful, but in a trophy housewife kind of way. It was judgy of me, but her smile didn't reach her eyes.

I took a step closer to Macey and reached out my hand. "Hello, I'm Sawyer."

She took my hand limply. "Oh. Sawyer, as in Tom Sawyer? That's cute. I'm Charlotte."

I lifted a brow. "More like Diane Sawyer. You probably don't know who she is."

She gave me a half dismissive nod, but her attention was on Macey.

"We should probably find our seats. The play starts soon." Macey was completely ignoring the woman in her path.

"You're right. We're in everyone's way." I looked at the clock above the bar. We had plenty of time, but something told me to get Macey away from this woman. Not that she needed saving, but because I didn't want this night to be ruined by somebody not-so-nice from her past. I gently pulled her away from the bottleneck we created by stopping in the middle of the aisle. "Nice to meet you," I said without looking back at Charlotte. I found our seats and didn't ask who that woman was, but I was dying to find out.

"So, that was my ex-girlfriend."

"I figured. She gave off a bad vibe. Pretty girl, but intense," I said.

Kris Bryant

Macey gave a half snort. "Very intense. Let's just say she was hard to shake after the breakup."

"Ouch. How long ago was that?" I asked.

"About two years ago."

"Dare I ask what happened?"

"She wasn't the person I thought she was, and I wasn't the person she wanted me to be."

"What did she want from you?"

Macey shrugged. "The fairy tale, and I was too busy working. She went into the relationship knowing I wasn't available every day but tried hard to get me home early every night. Guilt trips, breakdowns, and lots of tears."

"Sounds very manipulative. Did she live with you?"

"No, but she was always at my place. I'd never met anyone more desperate to get married than her," Macey said.

"Huh. Interesting because in my head I pictured her as a trophy wife," I said.

The lights flickered above, interrupting our conversation as people swarmed around us to get to their seats. I hated that I didn't get more information out of Macey before the play started. I would have to wait until at least intermission, but even then I wasn't sure I wanted to bring up an ex-girlfriend on date night.

"Thank you for bringing me here. I miss fun things like this," Macey whispered before the curtains opened. She held my hand and rested her head on my shoulder for a few seconds. I wondered if Charlotte saw us, but all of that was quickly forgotten once the play started. I knew what to expect since I'd seen it before, but watching Macey's face light up at different times and how she clapped enthusiastically after certain numbers made the experience better. It was almost as much fun watching her as it was watching what was happening onstage. When intermission came, I excused myself to go to the bathroom. It was as though I had a tracker on me, because Charlotte made a beeline for me the second I stepped into the bathroom.

"Are you and Macey together?" she asked.

I bristled. The hair on the back of my neck stood up. I continued to wash my hands while I came up with a suitable answer that wasn't rude like "mind your own fucking business" or one that would make her stomp up to Macey and demand answers. Honestly, we were dating but were we officially together? "I don't know who you are or why you think you need any information on her, but you need to leave us alone. I know about you." I didn't really, but I wasn't about to let her rudeness win.

"Are you exclusive?" She moved into my personal space as though to intimidate me.

I dried my hands, checked my makeup in the mirror, and turned to her so that our bodies and faces were only a few inches apart. I smirked because I was taller in my heels. I could hear her breathing ramp up. "I don't see how that's any of your business." I looked at the giant ring on her left hand. "Looks like you're taken anyway." She leaned back and I smiled slyly. "Have a good rest of your evening, Christie."

"Charlotte."

"Whatever." I opened the door and made my way back to our seats feeling as though I just slayed a dragon to save the day.

"Everything okay?" Macey asked.

I relaxed my body, realizing I was still on edge from the ridiculous encounter in the bathroom. I wasn't going to tell her. I had high hopes for this evening that didn't involve Charlotte. I held her hand. "It's great. Just a lot of people squeezed into a tiny space."

"The bathroom situation in these beautiful old theaters is ridiculous. I hope you give your employees equal amounts of space," Macey said.

"Gender neutral. I've already figured it out. Four private stalls, with sinks and mirrors in a shared space in front of them. Saw it at a restaurant downtown and loved the concept."

"That's great. I know the hospital has single gender-neutral bathrooms. That makes me happy."

I wondered if Macey had queer friends or colleagues. I was sure the hospital had a ton of queer employees, but she never talked about anyone. She never talked about friends, either. Just her family. I wanted to ask questions, but the lights flickered again and the second half of the play was going to start soon. My inquisition would have to wait until the drive home. When the play ended, the crowd stood and applauded for several minutes.

"This was incredible. Thank you for taking me," Macey said.

She surprised me by kissing me softly in front of everyone. I was giddy and floating as we made our way to the car. "Are you hungry?" I asked. It was ten, and late to grab dinner somewhere, but we could always find a drive-through.

"I have a few things at my place that we can heat up," Macey said.

I didn't hesitate. "I'm in." We spent the ride home talking about the play—what we liked most, what we thought made a social impact, and our favorite songs. In a massive surprise, Macey belted out a few lines from one of the songs. "Wow. You have an amazing voice. You told me you couldn't sing."

"When did I say that?" she asked. She was frowning and seemingly recalling all our conversations in her head. Shit, I did it again. She had a horrible voice in my dream world. I scrambled, praying I wasn't blowing my chances tonight.

"I thought you said something when Arya was singing at Tamsyn's." I remember they were talking about voices.

"I didn't realize you were listening to us," she said.

"It's kind of hard to not pay attention to you."

She gave me a look that made me accelerate. Since the accident, I'd been driving the speed limit. I pushed the car the extra five miles per hour, which would give us maybe thirty extra seconds, but a lot could happen in those thirty seconds.

"How does a grilled cheese sandwich sound?" Macey asked when she unlocked the front door.

Not what I had in mind, but I was far from tired so I rolled with it. "Sounds perfect. Put me to work," I said.

"Absolutely not. You're my guest. Have a seat and talk to me. Anything on your mind?" she asked.

Of course I was going to bring up Charlotte. "So, tell me the story about your lovely ex-girlfriend."

"Oh. Her." She rolled her eyes and washed her hands before pulling out the ingredients for our late dinner. "She's a nurse."

"Scandal at the hospital!" I said. Macey gave me a look and I pulled an imaginary zipper shut across my lips.

"Not much to say really. She wanted more than I could give her, and when I ended things with her, she didn't like it," Macey said. I pictured a cooked bunny on the stove from *Fatal Attraction* and waited for an equally horrific story.

"I had to change the locks on my doors, get a new code for my garage, and cancel her code for the gate. She had a hard time letting go."

I couldn't keep quiet. "She sounds like a nightmare."

"We had a slight stalker situation after we broke up and I made a promise to myself that I would never date somebody like her again."

My mouth dropped open. Macey was making gourmet grilled cheese and talking as if something as emotionally draining as a stalker wasn't a big thing. "I'm so sorry, Macey." I wanted to say something like I wouldn't do that to her, but that sounded like what a stalker would say.

"And was that the first time you've seen her since the breakup?"

She thinly sliced a tomato and added it to the sandwich. "No, I saw her about eighteen months ago. I believe she's married now. I don't look for her on socials so I don't know, nor do I care."

"She was wearing quite the ring, so that's probably true." I debated if I should tell her about our encounter in the bathroom and decided against it. I was selfish and I wanted a nice night with her. "Glad she's not in your life anymore. Did she work with you?"

"No. She worked in the maternity ward. She loves children

and was really pressing for a commitment from me so that we could start a family."

I pictured Charlotte kidnapping a newborn from the nursery and somehow getting away with it. "Were you that far along in your relationship?" We were just getting started and I couldn't imagine even bringing up babies with her.

"She thought it was more than it was. I felt pressured into it. It wasn't a nurturing relationship. I didn't appreciate her pushing me to like the things she did or do the same things she did. She didn't appreciate my individuality, and that's important to me. She wanted to blend into this power couple, but that meant giving up too much of myself."

"Well, I'm glad it's over. Or else I wouldn't be here. Good riddance." I'd heard enough of scary Charlotte. "What did you add to the butter? It smells delicious." I watched her expertly flip the golden-brown bread squares and straighten them on the griddle.

"A blend of Italian spices. It gives it a kick."

"I can't believe we're in your kitchen at almost eleven o'clock eating grilled cheese sandwiches," I said.

She put a sandwich in front of me and sat across the table. "I'm sorry we didn't have time to get dinner beforehand."

I touched her hand. "No worries. This just makes it more special. I mean, you remember the dates that don't go according to plan more than you remember the ones that do." I was going to remember this night for a long time. I was officially my own boss with my own business, had a beautiful woman on my arm at the theater, experienced an unfortunate run-in with her unhinged ex-girlfriend, and was now eating a grilled cheese sandwich by candlelight. It was the perfect night with just the right amount of angst, excitement, and sexiness. And I ended up with the girl.

"Finish up. I'm going to grab a bottle of wine. I'll meet you in the living room." She popped the last bite into her mouth, wiggled her eyebrows, and left the table. I quickly followed her after refilling my ice water. I checked my reflection in the large mirror on the wall on my way to the living room. Thankfully, I still looked good, but tired. It was a long week. I set my glass on the low coffee table and sank into the soft leather couch. She shook her hair loose from the hair tie and kicked off her shoes. It was hard not to stare at her perfect cleavage when she leaned down to place her heels on the side of the couch.

"In case I forgot to tell you, you look beautiful tonight."

"Thank you. Anything to get out of that drabby white coat," she said. The way she looked at me over the rim of her wine glass made my pulse jump. The air between us was instantly filled with excitement and silent promises.

I took a sip of water and watched as her gaze traveled my body. She didn't hide her appreciation, and that boosted my confidence. She made me feel sexy in a way I'd never felt before. Tonight was just getting started, and I couldn't wait to see how it ended up.

CHAPTER FOURTEEN

Y ou seem really far away," Macey said. She put her glass on the coffee table near mine and moved closer.

I lifted my eyebrow and smiled. "I'm within reach," I said.

She held out her hand. "I'm reaching, then."

I thought she was going to straddle me like she had before, but tonight she leaned back and pulled me on top of her. My dress crept up my thighs and I didn't even care. I slipped off my shoes before sinking into her and found her lips immediately. It was a slow, deep kiss that sent tiny jolts to every sensitive part of my body. I pressed closer. She moaned and ran her hands up and down my back. I broke the kiss long enough to tell her what I was thinking. She blinked several times and frowned as though not kissing her was the worst thing I could've done at that moment.

"This couch is lovely. It's soft, has a good bounce to it, and I already have very nice memories, but this isn't where I want to be," I said.

A slow dawning smile spread across her supple lips. "Where do you want to be?" she asked.

"Very much in this exact position, only not here."

She ran her thumb on my bottom lip. I briefly sucked it into my mouth. Her eyes narrowed with want. "I know where we can go," she said.

I kissed her swiftly before pulling her up from the couch.

She kept hold of my hand and walked to the primary bedroom. It was my first time being in the room. The first time I visited, she pointed and said her bedroom was down the hallway, but the tour stopped short. I wasn't ready then, but I was ready now. "This is a beautiful room and not at all how I re—" I quickly corrected myself. "Not what I expected."

The décor was mid-century American and a completely different style than the rest of the house. The low-profile bed had a headboard with alcoves on either side of the mattress to serve as nightstands. Macey looked at her reflection in the mirror as she slipped off the small silver hoop earrings and placed them in her jewelry box that sat on top of a rosewood lowboy dresser.

"Oh, is that a good thing or bad thing?" she asked. She turned and leaned her body against the dresser.

I casually made my way over to her and put my hands on either side of her. "It's a beautiful room, but I didn't come here to talk about your décor."

She looked down at my lips then back up to my eyes. "What did you come here for?" she asked.

I ran my fingertips up her arms and slipped my finger under the strap of her dress. I leaned forward and placed a small kiss on her collarbone before sliding the strap down her shoulder. "I came for you. I came for this. I came to show you how much you mean to me and how special you are." My lips trailed up her smooth neck. I could feel her pulse under my lips and smiled at how it fluttered faster and faster when I hit a sensitive spot. The tender spot behind her ear, along her jawline, until I finally pressed my lips against her full, luscious mouth.

She moaned and pulled me flush against her. The dresser wobbled from the force. I stepped backward with her in my arms, until I felt the mattress hit the back of my legs. I sat and held her hips in front of me until she realized I didn't want her to fall back with me. With both shoulder straps down, it was just a matter of unzipping the dress.

I twirled my finger in a circle. "Turn around."

She lifted her eyebrow and obliged. I ran my hands over her curves and found the zipper pull. I gave it a small tug and slowly watched as her form-fitting dress spread open to reveal even softer skin and no bra or panties. I gasped in surprise. She looked at me over her shoulder.

"I don't like lines when I wear tight dresses."

I nodded but couldn't say anything for fear that my heart would leap out of my throat where it currently resided. I turned her to face me so she could let the dress fall when she was ready. She didn't hesitate. I held my breath as gravity slid it down her body into a silky mess that pooled around her feet.

"I know I've said you're beautiful a thousand times, but I wasn't prepared for perfection, too." I didn't know where my words were coming from. I wasn't sappy or romantic, but something about this moment reminded me so much of my dream world that I couldn't help but combine the two. "And no tattoos."

She put her hands on my shoulders and motioned me to scoot back on the bed. "Was that a dealbreaker or something?"

I stalled for a moment. "Absolutely not. I always wondered if you had them."

I quickly pulled up my dress when I realized she was going to straddle me. I felt her heat and silky wetness on my thighs. When people said they didn't know if they were dreaming in the tender moments before sex, I finally understood what they meant. This was heaven. I cupped her breasts and ran my tongue in the valley between them. She threw her head back and put her hands on my knees. Macey wasn't a shy lover. Her body language told me exactly what she wanted. I sucked one nipple and pinched the other. She gasped her pleasure and pushed my head into her breast until I sucked harder.

"Yes. Just like that."

The evidence of her arousal on my thigh was too hard to ignore. I reached down to stroke the swollen flesh that surrounded her clit and was rewarded with a deep moan and a hard kiss. It was difficult to penetrate her at this angle, but I wanted nothing more than to feel her slick, throbbing walls around my fingers. I wrapped my arm around her waist and flipped her so she was underneath me. She spread her legs and pushed my hand down to her pussy. She was bold and sexy and when I entered her, she kept eye contact with me. Pleasure washed over her and her skin flushed with growing passion. Her back arched with fulfillment as I moved inside her. I was gentle at first, but her thrusting hips into my hand told me she wanted more. I added a third finger and waited until she relaxed enough to allow me to move. She was wet, throbbing, and her entire body tensed against mine begging for release. She was addictive. I couldn't get enough of her. I slid down her body, keeping my fingers inside, and moved them slowly when my mouth found her clit. She was hard and smooth and the second my tongue licked it, she grabbed the sheets with both fists.

"Oh my God, Sawyer."

Hearing her say my name empowered me. I was giving this woman as much pleasure as she could take and I had barely even started. I vowed by the end of the night, Macey would think of ways to make me stay. I smiled as she groaned her frustration when I pulled out. She was stretched enough for me to slip right back inside. I did that several times until her legs started shaking. I was rewarded with several pulsating gushes as she cried out in pleasure. That had never happened to me before while having sex, and the aches in my arm and my neck magically disappeared as she clutched me with every wave. She covered her face with her arms and took deep, long breaths. I pulled out carefully and rolled her on top of me. She rested her head on my shoulder. I held her close and tried hard not to smile smugly or say something completely inappropriate or awkward. Every time words sat on my lips ready to change the mood of the moment, I pressed them together and waited in silence.

"That was unexpected," she said.

I couldn't stop the smile from spreading. Sex with Macey was better than I expected or dreamed of. I wanted to laugh gleefully, but I was trying to behave like an adult. "I wasn't sure if you came." She leaned up and looked at me like I was bonkers.

"My bedding is soaked. We're going to have to move to one of the guest rooms."

Her cheeks were flushed and her curly hair was damp along her forehead and temples. There was a slight sheen across her upper lip. Even a sweaty mess, I'd never seen anyone more beautiful. The real Macey was vibrant, but also matter-of-fact. I wanted to talk about what just happened, but she was hell-bent on moving to another bed. It didn't occur to me that maybe she was embarrassed.

"We could stay on this side," I said.

She dropped a quick kiss on my lips and crawled out of bed. "Absolutely not. Follow me," she said and held out her hand.

I grabbed it and followed her to the next room. She was extremely comfortable naked whereas I was trying to push my dress down and not fall as it was twisted weirdly around my knees and across my breasts. I stepped out of it before falling onto the bed with her to pick back up where we left off. The minute her lips found mine, I'd forgotten about everything except wanting to touch her and be touched by her. This time, I kissed my way down her body and held her hips while running my tongue up and down her slit. She wiggled against me for friction and I realized foreplay wasn't her thing. She wanted to orgasm. I gave her exactly what she wanted. I wasn't gentle. I spread her lips apart and licked and sucked until she pulled my hair and came loudly. It was extremely enjoyable, but I missed the tenderness of dream Macey.

"What are you thinking about?" she asked.

Worst question to ever ask somebody after sex. I was still between her legs with my head resting on her thigh.

"Sex," I answered honestly.

She laughed and tucked my hair behind my ear. I flipped it over my shoulder in case it was tickling her sensitive skin.

"I'm sorry about earlier," she said.

"Why? It was amazing." Everything was great except the part where she quickly jumped up and practically jogged to another room.

She shrugged. "It's embarrassing even though I know it's perfectly normal. I didn't want that to happen our first time."

I leaned up on my elbows. "I want that to happen every time. That means I did something right and you enjoyed it immensely."

Another delightful laugh. "I definitely did. Both times."

I was ready for round three. My body was tense, wanting to find my own orgasm, but I wanted to find out what she liked the most and keep doing it. I knew that it would only take a few soft strokes before I came. Tonight was about her. I stroked the soft skin of her thighs, marveling at their smoothness. She spread her legs open for better access. I brushed my finger across her clit and she jumped.

"I'm still sensitive there," she said.

"Do you want me to stop?" I asked.

"Not at all."

When I slipped two fingers inside, the moan that pushed through her lips made my body weak. It was deep and guttural, and I wanted to hear it over and over. Sex with the real Macey was beyond incredible.

"Just like that."

Her body was hot to the touch and her insides were liquid fire. I slid in and out easily and added a third finger. Macey accepted the pleasure and moved her hips against my hand. I paced myself and watched as she rolled her hips and dug her heels into the mattress. She was slower this time but wanted the orgasm above all else. It was exciting, but in a different way. Dream Macey wasn't as bold and liked to cuddle after each crescendo. This woman was real and determined to come as many times as she could before her body gave out. Hearing her come for the third time made my heart and ego swell. Was I ever able to do that in such a short time before?

"Come here." Macey's intimate voice dripped with satisfaction. I climbed up her body and rolled to the side. She ran her fingertips up my arm, over my neck, and swiped her thumb across my lips. "You have the best mouth and not just during sex. It's always the first thing I notice about people, and I noticed yours right away."

"What do you like about it?" I asked.

"Your lips. Besides the whole 'they're capable of great pleasure,' I like the color, the shape, and how kissable they are," she said.

I melted. This was what I wanted. Sweet talk after sex. "That's funny. I've always liked your lips, too. They're so full and soft."

"I always thought my lips were too big," she said.

"Oh, no. They are suckable. Especially the bottom one." To prove my point, I sucked her bottom lip into my mouth and gently scraped my teeth over it.

"I don't think suckable is a word," she said.

"Suckly? No, that doesn't work either. I'm sticking with suckable. I think we should make it a word even if it isn't."

Macey rolled onto her side and trailed her fingers over my chest and gently pinched my hardened nipples. "These are suckable." She leaned over to prove her point. I gasped when her teeth grazed the areola before sucking it into her mouth.

"Suckable," I said through gritted teeth. It was a pleasure-pain experience and heightened my already sensitive body.

She spread my legs apart with her knees and moved her lips back up to mine as her hand caressed the soft, tingly skin of my pussy. Just the tip of her finger rubbing along my slit had me nearly orgasming. When she finally sank her fingers inside, I let go. I bucked against her, desperate for release. Her mouth against mine and her knee pushing her fingers deeper inside sent me over the edge, and I fell into waves of pleasure. She didn't stop. She pushed her thumb against my clit and continued fucking me until I came again. I clutched her as every pulse of pleasure worked its way through my body. Sunset colors swirled behind my closed eyes. Red when her lips found my pleasure points, warm orange as her hands caressed my curves, and yellow at the joy of this moment. I didn't want this to end. I took deep breaths as I waited for my body to relax.

"Are you okay?"

I nodded. "I'm more than okay." I felt her briefly tense up when I snuggled closer. She put her arm around me and held me. No words were spoken after that. I barely remember her pulling up the covers before I crashed hard in her arms.

"Wake up, Sawyer."

I cracked an eyelid open to find Macey staring at me. I squeezed my eyes shut. Oh, fuck, I thought. Not again. This couldn't be happening again.

"Am I at Memorial?"

Macey leaned over me. "What are you talking about?"

I opened my eyes wider. "Wow. I must be really sleepy." I cleared my throat. My voice sounded raspy. "Come here." I scooped her up and nuzzled her soft neck. "Tonight was incredible. The way you let go. Sex with you was good before, but that was mind-blowing."

"Good before?"

"Yeah, that night you cooked spaghetti and pretended you couldn't cook." I thought I was losing my grip on her and it took me a few seconds before I realized she was trying to pull away. I lifted my head from the pillow and pushed my hair out of my face. "What? What's the matter?"

"Sawyer, tonight was the first night we had sex. We've never done this before." She stood and wrapped a blanket around her.

"That's not true," I said. I closed my eyes again and pulled her pillow into my arms because I missed her warmth and scent. "Your sheets smell like you." I heard her open drawers and close them forcefully. That got my attention. "What are you doing?"

"I'm going downstairs." She sounded agitated and stormed off.

My mind was fuzzy. What was happening? I slid out of bed

and slipped my dress over my head and twisted my hair back. My shoes were probably downstairs. I splashed water on my face to help wake me up. As I stared at my reflection it finally dawned on me what I had done. Panic turned my blood cold. I quickly patted my face dry and made my way downstairs. Macey was sitting on the couch in the dark. "I'm sorry, Macey."

"You should probably go. I'm not in the mood to talk and I think we both need to take a step back," she said.

My heart felt like a cannonball in my chest. "I understand. Again, I'm sorry." I was going to say I was working on myself and I didn't want to miss out on time with her, but I quietly grabbed my shoes and clutch and walked out the front door. I deserved that. I was angry at myself for fucking things up. I knew Ladybug Junction wasn't real, but why was my brain so hung up on a place that didn't exist?

CHAPTER FIFTEEN

I know the difference between a dream and reality. At least I think I do."

Kerri sat with her legs crossed and her fashionable glasses perched high up on the bridge of her nose. "Why are you questioning it? Did something happen this weekend?"

I fell back on the couch and stared up at the ceiling. It felt really weird talking to her about my sex life with Macey since she knew her. Was that a conflict of interest? She assured me everything was confidential and didn't interfere with her professional relationship with Dr. Burr. I had no choice but to believe her.

"I did it again. I mixed up my worlds."

"What happened?"

Kerri folded her hands in her lap and waited patiently for me to spill my guts.

"Everything was great. We went to see *Hamilton* and then went back to her house for a late dinner. Eventually, we ended up in bed and I woke up thinking we were in dream world. I mixed them up again." I stood and started pacing. "I keep doing it, only this time she got mad and I left very awkwardly in the middle of the night." I groaned and smacked my palm on my forehead. One minute we were cuddling in postcoital bliss, and the next she was storming off.

"Do you want to talk about why you're doing that? Why you're mixing up the two?"

"Isn't that why I'm here? To sort this out?" I was frustrated. I'd been to therapy for months and I always thought that was the goal all along. Kerri and I were on different pages.

"Why do you think you're doing that?"

I shrugged. "I don't know. Macey in dream world has all the qualities I'm looking for."

"What about the Macey you're dating here?" Kerri asked.

It was a valid question. "She's wonderful. She's smart, beautiful, and very career-oriented."

"Does she have any qualities that you don't like?"

I knew I had to be honest. If Kerri was going to help me, I needed to answer truthfully. I closed my eyes and thought hard. "She's standoffish sometimes. And she works a lot. We don't do the weekend dating. It's more of whenever we have a free moment."

"Does not having a schedule bother you?" she asked.

"Not really because I know I'm going to be super busy with my new practice," I said. I sat down again.

"Since our time is almost up, I have an exercise for your journal. Make a list in your journal of qualities you like in yourself and qualities you'd like to improve. Bring it in, and we can discuss it next time," she said.

"Do you think it'll help?" I asked. We'd had maybe a dozen sessions, and while I knew issues weren't going to be solved overnight, I was hoping for more defined answers instead of more questions.

She assured me that we were making progress. "Sometimes the strangest avenues put us on the right track," she said.

I couldn't help myself. "Sounds like something you read off a fortune cookie."

She laughed. "Sometimes they make sense. I'll see you Thursday."

I avoided all places in the hospital where I might run into

Macey. The other night was nothing short of a disaster. I sent an apology text the next day and she said something noncommittal back, but the vibe was off.

I sneaked out a side door and walked to the parking lot. I was a coward. I sat in my car and let the tears fall. I was angry. I was angry that my mind was playing tricks on me, angry that I was blowing it with a wonderful person, and scared that I was walking away from a secure job to one that might fail. It was a lot to take in. Kerri and I spent two sessions discussing the good and bad of my new career path, and even though I felt good about it then, doubt was starting to creep into the cracks.

I headed back to work even though there wasn't a lot for me to do. Oliver had hired two veterinarians. One just graduated college in May, and the other was somebody he knew from his hometown. He paid his relocation fee, which I was sure was thousands of dollars. The recent graduate, Rowan Kent, was shadowing me until my last day. He was an eager learner and asked a lot of questions. Oliver reminded me that I wasn't allowed to tell any clients I was opening my own practice. He knew that I could easily get over half of the clients to move over to my practice, and that scared him.

"Hello, Byron. Are you ready for me to look at your stitches?" I asked. "We might be able to take them out today." I scratched the chihuahua softly behind his ears and was rewarded with kisses.

"If you don't do it, he will."

His owner rushed him here ten days ago after he was attacked by a neighbor's dog. I couldn't remember how many stitches I gave him, but it was quite a few for such a little dog. He looked at me so trustingly. I spent several moments scratching his chin and rubbing his ears to get him relaxed before I touched the bandage. I didn't care how long it took us to do this. Rowan was going to learn that being kind to owner and pet was the best customer service. Plus, the kid was still fresh and it was about saving the animals with him, not about how much you could bill the owners. I carefully unwrapped the self-adhesive bandage that circled Byron's back and around his belly and checked the progress. His owner did a good job of applying ointment because the stitches looked clean and healthy.

"I'm going to leave these two stitches in because the skin hasn't completely healed, but the rest can come out. He won't be able to reach them with his mouth or his hind legs." I had Rowan hold him steady while I inspected and removed twenty-one stitches. "You're such a good boy." I checked for any infections and left the two stitches in place. "Just bring him back in three days and we'll get him in and take these out."

"Should I ask for you?" she asked.

"I don't know if I'm on the schedule, but Rowan will be able to remove them. He's one of our new doctors."

"Oh, are you all expanding?" she asked.

I looked at Rowan and thought, fuck it. If he told Oliver, he told Oliver. "Rowan is one of the doctors hired to replace me. I'm leaving Oliver Strong at the end of the month."

"What? Where are you going?" the client asked.

"I'm pursuing other interests. He'll be well taken care of regardless of who helps. I promise you," I said.

"Well, good luck in your other interests." Bryon's owner winked at me. I smiled. She was one client I could count on. I knew there would be others once word got out.

"Thank you," I said.

The patients in the waiting room were listed in order of need. I let Rowan call the next one, Duke, a four-year-old Shih Tzu, who swallowed a bouncy ball. This was going to be tricky, and time was of the essence. "What do you recommend, Doctor?"

Rowan looked almost as scared as Duke's owners.

"What size ball?" he asked.

One of the owners retrieved another bouncy ball from his pocket and handed it to me. "It's this size."

I looked at the size and realized it was too large to safely pass. "How long ago did this happen?"

"About twenty minutes."

I was super pissed that Oliver or Meredith didn't take this case immediately. This was an emergency situation. I kept my emotions in check. "Rowan? Any thoughts?" I didn't want to call the kid out like that, but he was shadowing me to learn the way we practice here.

"X-ray of the abdomen to see how far along it is," he said.

"That's a good idea. We can also induce vomiting, and if that doesn't work, endoscopy is an option." I turned to the concerned owners. "We're going to take him back and give him something that will make him vomit. Hopefully, it comes up. If it doesn't, we'll look at other options. Like Dr. Kent said, we might have to do an x-ray and scope him to try to get it out."

"How much will that cost?"

"It depends. Let's take it one step at a time. You can have a seat in the waiting room and we'll keep you posted," I said.

"Apomorphine?" Rowan asked.

"You got it. This is the fun part."

Duke wasn't excited about the medicine. I didn't blame him. It smelled bad and I couldn't imagine what it tasted like. I had Rowan wait with Duke in the room while I helped one of the techs with a nail trim and shots on a blue-eyed husky who howled the whole time. By the time I got back to the room, Duke had puked up the ball and Rowan was doing his best to not be grossed out by the stains on his clothes. He was going to fit in nicely with Oliver and Meredith.

"Oh, great! It came out." I washed the ball and slipped it into a clear baggie while Rowan changed his jacket and one of the techs cleaned the room. I handed the bag to Rowan. "Let's tell them the good news." Duke was lethargic but wagged his fluffy tail when he saw his parents.

"How much did that cost?"

I shook my head. Not a "thank God he's okay" or "thank you for helping him" but a snide comment about money. "Less than an x-ray or an endoscopy." I let Rowan explain everything and moved on to the next patient. I had a steady flow the rest of the afternoon, so when Tamsyn's text came right before my shift ended, I finally relaxed but instantly tensed when I read it.

Don't forget to bring a salad. Macey's already committed to dessert. I'll see you at six thirty.

Macey was still going? I hadn't told Tamsyn about the latest incident. *Yes, boss. See you later.* She would know the moment we all shared space that something was off. I slipped off my white coat and said good night to the crew. I didn't have enough time to go home and grab a salad, so I ordered one from the Rabbit Hole to be delivered by the time I got to Tamsyn's.

I slipped into nice shorts and a clean top. Thanks to my loose work schedule over the summer, I spent more time at Tamsyn's pool and had a nice tan to show off. I threw my hair back, slipped on sandals, and hustled out the door. Still driving the speed limit, I arrived right on time, right when the salad did, and a few minutes after Macey. I grabbed the salad from the delivery guy and walked into the house.

"I'm here." I said it loud enough for the whole house to hear.

"We're out back," Tamsyn yelled.

No matter what was going on between us, I couldn't help but smile when I saw Macey. The fluttering in my stomach was real, regardless of anything else. I knew that was real. "Hi." I handed Tamsyn the salad and kissed her cheek. Arya waved from her inflatable unicorn from the pool and Lauren gave me a quick hug.

"It's good to see you," Macey said.

There was a slight hesitation on how Macey and I were supposed to greet, but she held open her arms and I walked into her hug. Her body felt warm from the sun and she smelled like lavender. My fingers briefly stroked the soft skin of her back.

"It's good to see you, too," I said.

Macey was sweet and cordial and offered the seat next to hers. I ignored Tamsyn's lifted brow and sat.

"How was work?" Macey asked.

"It was fine. One of the new recruits, Rowan, is shadowing

me this week and learned that sometimes the most expensive solution isn't the best. I'm sure that goes against Oliver's rule."

She covered my hand with hers. "I'm sure spending the time with you is worth a lot. Rowan will learn so much from you."

My temperature spiked at her touch. "I can't wait to hear about how many times he tries to get more money out of people and fails."

"What can I get you to drink?" Tamsyn asked.

"What are you drinking?" I asked Macey and pointed at her fruity looking cocktail.

"It's virgin. I'm on call."

"I'll have what she's drinking, only not virgin." I needed the alcohol to settle my nerves. We hadn't had a good conversation since I left her house at two in the morning last week. I knew now wasn't the time, but we needed clarity. "We've talked about my day. How was yours?"

"One of my patients made big strides. It's always nice to see progress, especially when you're not expecting it so soon," she said. She had a dreamy, faraway look in her eyes, and I knew it was a good day. I also knew she couldn't talk about specifics.

"That's great," I said.

"Auntie Macey. Come help me out of the pool, please." Arya was trying to paddle to the side with one tiny arm. She could've easily swum to the side, but new adults were around and Arya loved attention. I gaped dramatically at Arya.

"What? Have you replaced me already? I was only ten minutes late."

"She's your girlfriend. It's okay."

Macey walked over to the pool to help Arya. Tamsyn pounced. She slid into Macey's vacated spot.

"What's going on?"

I played innocent. "What do you mean?"

"Don't give me that. Something's going on. What is it?" She pressed.

I stalled, hoping to give Macey enough time to make her

way back, but she was taking her time playing with Arya. "I did the thing again."

"Sawyer…"

Tamsyn's drew my name out.

"We had a really nice night, but then I fucked it up. Let's talk about it later. I want to enjoy our time," I said. I pointed to Macey, who was playing with Arya. "She's so good with her."

"I mean, my kid is adorable, too," Tamsyn said.

"Without a doubt," I said.

"I wonder why Macey never had any kids. Have you all talked about it?" Tamsyn asked.

"Career stuff, bad first marriage, you know, the usual," I said. I saw Tamsyn shake her head at me in disbelief.

"Apparently, we need to have a morning coffee with no one else around so you can fill me in. I barely know anything about her or you and her." I could feel her blue eyes boring into me, but I refused to look. "You've never been this private before," she said.

I noted the concern in her voice. "While this relationship is hot and exciting, it's also disturbing. I don't have peace with her." Tamsyn gave me a weird look. "It's hard to explain. We'll talk about it later. I'll stop by your office tomorrow before work with coffee." I turned my attention to Macey and Arya.

"We can stream the new mermaid movie after dinner if anyone is interested," I said.

"Can we watch it while we eat?" Arya asked.

Tamsyn checked the time. "Come out of the pool and put on some dry clothes. The sooner we start eating, the sooner we can turn it on."

By the time Arya was changed and in the dining room, dinner was ready.

"I love the family you have here," Macey said.

"Me, too," Tamsyn said.

"When Donna and Bill join us, it's a party," Lauren said.

"My parents," I explained.

Macey nodded. "I remember them. Very sweet, and they love you very much."

Guilt washed over me because I'd forgotten to call or visit them this week. "They've always supported me."

"It really helps when you have a supportive family," Macey said.

I had yet to meet any of Macey's family, but she only met mine because I was in the hospital. I was excited about meeting them, but after our last encounter, I figured our relationship took a few steps back. "I appreciate mine so much."

"I'm done. Can we watch the movie now?" Arya asked. She pointed to her almost empty plate.

"Yes, but turn it low. We're still eating," Lauren said. She wiped Arya's mouth first before sending her into the other room.

"She's so adorable," Macey said. "How's the school year going? She's in the second grade?"

Macey was so smooth around people that for a moment I thought we were okay. When we finished and joined Arya in the living room, she sat in a wingback chair, reminding me that we weren't. I sat on the couch next to Arya, and Tamsyn and Lauren were snuggling on the love seat. The vibe was weird, and by the end of the movie, my anxiety was at a ten. I didn't know what was going on with us.

"Let's get you to bed. Say good night."

Tamsyn carted Arya around the room, and she and Lauren excused themselves to tuck her in bed. That left me and Macey alone. "Do you want to go for a walk? I feel like we need to talk," I said.

"I feel like we do, too."

My heart felt like it dropped in my chest. I'd screwed up too many times. I dreaded this moment because deep down, it felt like it was over between us.

CHAPTER SIXTEEN

I sent Tamsyn a quick message telling her the plan in case she wondered where we were and followed Macey outside.

"This is a nice neighborhood," she said.

I fell into step beside her. "I always talked about moving here one day, but it's a neighborhood that's designed with families in mind."

Macey crossed her arms in front of her to ward off the slight chill in the air. I didn't even notice the drop in temperature. "I live in one of those neighborhoods, too."

I gave her a doubtful look. Her house was in a gated community, and even though I'd been to her house only a few times, I'd never seen a child outside playing. This neighborhood was dotted with children playing on swing sets, swimming in pools, riding their bikes, and playing ball in the park across the street.

"You have a beautiful house," I said. I lived in a neighborhood of young professionals and older, retired women. My townhouse was almost too big for me, but Macey's house was at least three times the size of mine.

"So, what are you thinking about?" she asked.

"I want to know where we stand." I was careful not to overshare and paused to allow the conversation to happen organically.

"I really like you and I enjoy spending what little time we have together. I just don't know if we're in the right place to date," she said.

Her words hurt. A lot, but I understood. "I don't disagree, but can you give me your reasons?"

She stopped and placed one hand on her waist and the other on her forehead. "I know this is going to sound awful, but you really need to work out the fantasy me versus the real me. I got out of two bad relationships because they wanted to change me or thought I was somebody else, and I feel like our relationship is headed that way."

I took a deep, fluttery breath. I knew we needed to be honest, but I also didn't want to say good-bye. I wasn't ready to let go. "I understand, but I don't want to just walk away. I'm working on self-improvements and understanding why my dream world, which only lasted a few days, is dominating my reality."

She put her hand on my arm. "I'm happy you are taking the right steps. You went through a very traumatic experience and that trumps so many things. The brain is a beautiful organ, but it sure likes to scramble things up." At my horrified look, she quickly added, "I'm sure you'll get it all sorted out."

I bit down on my bottom lip to act as though I was thinking about everything, but I was trying to stop the tears from falling. I hated feeling like this, I hated not knowing what was happening in my head and in my heart. "I'm sure it's best that we cool it. I mean, I have a lot going on and so do you." My parents would have worked through it though. That's what you did in a relationship that was worth it. I felt my shoulders drop in defeat. We weren't on the same page.

"I think you're so kind, generous, smart, and ambitious. I love that you are starting your own practice. You have all the qualities I admire in a person," she said.

I'd never had somebody break up with me so smoothly. Just the other day we talked about how we never talked to our ex-partners. I wanted to fight for us, but I also wanted to see therapy through and figure out the mystery of my hold on my dream world. "Thank you." I didn't want to say "same" or "ditto," but those words would've worked better than me blurting out the truth.

"Do you think Kerri is helping?"

We were almost back to Tamsyn's house, so we slowed our pace. "She's helping. I know it's a process, but I wish there was a pill I could take and everything would be back to normal."

"Hopefully, you'll get answers soon," Macey said.

She held my hand until we got to her car. I leaned against the passenger door and looked into her eyes. Was she really doing this to us? Could I fix myself and put Ladybug Junction behind me and accept the real Macey, who was equal parts amazing and wonderful?

"Some things make sense and I've dealt with them pretty well."

"Oh, I agree," she said.

"I feel like I know you so well even though it's only been a few months," I said.

"The week you were in the hospital, I spent a lot of time in your room. I ended my nights finishing up paperwork for the staff."

I smiled. "I didn't know that."

"True story. You were always my last patient. Staying in your room was a great way to check on you, spend time with you, and have a quiet place to finish my paperwork without interruptions. Nobody discovered my secret hiding place, well, except for my family," she said.

"I feel so used," I joked. It was the first time we laughed together all night. It was also the first time she shared that information with me.

"You were so easy to talk to then and now," she said.

"You talked to me?" I asked.

"Every night and every time I visited you on rounds," she said.

I closed my eyes and thought about what she said. "Like, what kinds of things did you tell me? Maybe things about your family? Like your aunt Abby or your brothers?" I clenched my jaw waiting for her to answer.

"Probably. I'm sure I took calls from my family. I was pretty much at the hospital the entire week because of you and two other patients I was concerned about," she said.

I put my hands on my knees to keep myself from sinking to the ground. "Don't you think that would have been really good information for me to know?"

"What do you mean?"

"Macey, I have been struggling, trying to separate reality from my dream world or whatever you want to call it because what you told me about your private life while I was in a coma is stuck in my brain. I've spent months trying to figure it out. Do you not get that?" I clenched my teeth and lowered my voice. "You knew I was having problems. Maybe you could have shared that information with me sooner? I mean, come on, you're a neuro doctor." I tapped my finger on my temple. "Did it never occur to you that had you just told me all of this sooner, I could be a lot further ahead in my therapy?"

She put her hands on her hips and stared at me. I was doing everything I could to not direct all my negative energy at her. I knew I had some responsibility in this mess.

"It never occurred to me that I could be part of the problem," she said in a low voice.

With her admission of some guilt, I allowed my anger to flow. I pushed off the car and walked around her to the sidewalk. "While I appreciate the after-hours care, maybe know for future patients that they might be able to hear you."

"I'm sorry, Sawyer. I always tell family members to talk to their loved ones in comas because there is a strong possibility their words are getting through. I just never thought the conversations I had over the phone would have such an impact on you."

I took a few steps closer to Tamsyn's house. "Well, at least now I have more to share with Kerri. Maybe that really important piece of information will speed things along. Have a good night, Macey." Even though I wanted to stomp off like an angry child, I turned on my heels and let myself into Tamsyn's. She didn't follow.

"How'd it go?" Tamsyn asked. She and Lauren were scrolling on their phones when I walked in.

"Unbelievable!" I threw up my hands and stomped over to the chair.

"I'm going to guess that's bad," Lauren said.

They both put their phones down and gave me their undivided attention.

"What happened?" Lauren asked.

"It's still very much my problem, but I just found out that when I was in my coma, Macey spent a lot of time in my room talking on the phone to her family and then talking to me. So, all this time I thought I was losing my mind, but I wasn't."

"Wait. Hold up. What does that mean?"

"It means that I'm not crazy. That I knew about her family like Aunt Abby and her brothers because she was having conversations in my room."

Tamsyn shook her head. "I'm still not following. Why is it her fault?"

I threw up my hands like everything was so obvious. "She could've told me she did this. That would've saved hours of therapy."

"But that's not the only thing you're struggling with, right?" Lauren asked.

"What do you mean?"

"One of your biggest problems is that you're trying to fit a circle into a square. You have this idea of who Macey is and she isn't that person. How do her phone calls and free chatter while you were in a coma explain that problem?" Lauren asked.

Tamsyn nodded. "When's your next therapy session?"

I slumped in the chair. "In two days."

"That's not too long of a wait. What she told you will totally help the process, but it's not the reason you're stuck there. You know?" Tamsyn said.

It was a knee-jerk reaction because she was dumping me and I wanted to be okay with it. Being mad at her protected my heart. "You're probably right."

"Did Macey leave?"

I felt bad, but not bad enough to chase after her. Lauren and Tamsyn didn't have all the information, but they brought up good points. "Yes. She told me to tell you all thank you for the invitation," I said. She really didn't, but she would've had I not just stormed off.

"First take care of you, and then worry about you and her," Tamsyn said. She pulled me into a hug and I finally let the tears fall. I didn't sob because I felt Macey and I weren't officially done. If I could get to Kerri and clear some of the dust in my mind, maybe I could find my way back to her.

❖

The session went so well that I was looking forward to our next session. I felt I was close to a breakthrough with the new information and a large piece of the puzzle finally snapping into place. Kerri was impressed at the number of connections I'd been able to make between my list and the real world. The act of doing that made the separation between my dream world and reality much easier to see. There was still a lot of work to be done, but I felt better at the progress we made.

When are you officially opening your business? Have you hired anyone yet?

Yara's text reminded me to head over to the clinic and check out the progress Jeremy and his crew had made. He promised they would be well ahead of the November first opening day. They could pull workers off different jobs if necessary, but he assured me they wouldn't be late.

November first but I'll start the interview process in a few weeks. I need another veterinarian and at least two technicians. Why? Do you know anyone who might be interested? She never hinted that she wanted to leave Oliver Strong. She told me that since I left, the flow was a little bumpy. Meredith was stressed because now she had to take the hard cases and it was wearing her thin. And Oliver was still in the office every day. She didn't think Rowan would last, but he was doing an okay job.

Honestly? I'd be up for a tech job if you'd consider me.

The smile on my face felt foreign, like I didn't deserve that happiness. *It's going to be chaos at the beginning. I'm still working on health benefits, but the job is yours if you want it.*

Hell yeah! I'm in.

Fantastic news. I'll send you over a contract tonight. I followed it with several celebratory emojis. Yara was my first employee. I quickly sent her another text. *If you know any other techs not from OS, and you can vouch for them, I'm in the market to hire two more.*

I know a few people. I'll get back to you.

This was turning out better than I expected. I could easily make Yara office manager if she wanted. My only concern was finding another veterinarian who was interested in a startup business. I had a job description that I could post to veterinary message boards. I could also look for recent graduates or people with a few years' experience on LinkedIn. Finding help was easy. Getting employees to stay was the hard part. I needed to offer something special like quarterly bonuses or profit-sharing. I was still making a mental list of things to do and ways to sweeten my employment offers when I pulled into the parking lot of Healing Paws. I sat in my car for about a minute just staring at the building and marveling at how well what I saw and helped design on paper was coming to life before my eyes. I was having a moment when my phone rang.

"Well, are you coming in or are you going to sit out there with that goofy grin on your face?"

I knew my mom was proud and excited to be on the journey with me. It also didn't surprise me that she was on site. Ever since construction began, she was at Healing Paws daily. At first it was just to drop off cold lemonade and warm cookies to the crew, but now she had a hard hat and was talking to Jeremy's foreman every day. "I'm just soaking it all in. The quiet before the storm, you know. See you in a minute."

"Soak it in, baby girl. It's a beautiful thing."

My phone rang as soon as I disconnected the call with my mom. It was Tamsyn.

"Hi. What are you doing?"

"Hiring people. What are you doing?"

"Oh! You have employees now? Since when?" she asked.

"Since about two minutes ago. Yara reached out and I hired her. And I asked her to tell anyone else she knew that I was looking for help. Except for the other people at Oliver Strong. She was the only one who was really good."

"That's great. Where are you now?"

"Just sitting in my car looking at my new business. Apparently, my mother thought it was creepy and told me to come inside."

"Have you had a chance to look at the e-blast?" Tamsyn asked.

"I haven't checked my mail but I will right now." I pulled up the envelope icon on my phone.

Lauren had designed a welcome to Healing Paws newsletter that she was going to blast to over two thousand people in the area. I didn't ask where she got the client list. Marketing was her job and she had a lot of contacts. I was sure she bought a list off the internet. My collaboration with the local Petco didn't start until opening day, but I had high hopes there as well. I was doing everything Oliver was not, but I believed my way was better. Oliver was old-school and didn't believe in the importance of social media. While his customer base was acceptable, it was almost exclusively word-of-mouth advertising. He didn't have to spend money on ads or work out deals with pet supply box stores. But I was hungry and needed income to filter in as soon as possible. Plus, I was educated on the latest and greatest treatments. While going to conventions interrupted my schedule, they paid off in the long run.

"I love it. Tell Lauren she did a great job." My new logo popped with bright colors and my heart grew when I read all the bullets of services Healing Paws provided that so many other clinics did not.

"If you find any changes, let me know. It's scheduled to blast a week before you open. Oh, and I've ordered bales of hay that Jeremy will deliver after the inspection. We don't want anything flammable there to prevent the doors from opening."

She was talking about our VIP celebration Tricks-for-Treats on October thirty-first, the day before I officially opened. I needed a grand autumn scene to be warm and welcoming. The hay bales would serve as additional seating and décor. I looked up to find my mom standing in the doorway with her arms folded across her chest.

"Shit, I have to go. I'll call you later." I paused because it sounded like I was ungrateful. "Listen. I owe you big. You've been my best friend through thick and thin. I couldn't have done this without you."

"I love you and I know you're going to be so successful. Tell Donna we love her and I'll talk to you later tonight," Tamsyn said.

I dabbed my eyes and tried to sound like I wasn't on the verge of tears. "Thanks. Bye." I quickly hung up and walked over to my mother. She hugged me and promptly handed me a hard hat. "How's it going today?"

She put her arm around my shoulders and steered me inside. "I think you're going to be so pleased with the progress."

CHAPTER SEVENTEEN

I dropped my journal on the table. The thud wasn't loud, but the information was explosive. "No way," I said. I crossed my arms across my chest and stared at Kerri.

"It's completely feasible," she said. She flipped back the pages of her notebook until she found what she was looking for. "Carefree, vibrant, beautiful, ambitious, risk-taker, special, involved with her community, loving family, and loyal." She waited for the words to sink in and flipped to one of the last entries. Her eyes scanned the page. "Loosen up, take risks, start my own business, have fun, live life, establish my community, and spend time with my family. Do you see the similarities?" She placed her notepad on the table and calmly folded her hands in her lap.

I rubbed my hands over my face and leaned forward, resting my elbows on my knees. I felt defeated. "So, the qualities I listed that attracted me to Macey in my dream world were really qualities I wanted to see in myself?"

"The lists are very similar."

"But it doesn't make sense," I said.

"Your accident happened at a time when you were very stressed at work. Isn't it possible that your mind created Ladybug Junction as a protective measure, giving you the opportunity to self-reflect during downtime, which in this case was your coma?"

I chewed on my lip as my mind processed the possibility of something so unbelievable. I shook my head even though I knew it to be true. "No. No. That can't be."

"It's a lot to take in," she said.

I nodded and checked the clock. We had ten minutes left. I wasn't sure if I wanted the time or to leave immediately. To say I was overwhelmed was an understatement. "What now?"

"Whatever you need," she said.

After the soft breakup with Macey over two weeks ago, I was slowly starting to come to terms with my life. It was time to accept that we were probably over and move on. A lot of my questions about my coma experience had been answered. Now I had to process the truth. It was liberating but also kind of sad. Ladybug Junction was my cocoon. "I have a lot to think about."

Kerri handed me a note with the name of a book. "This has good material about how the brain changes and heals. Now would probably be a good time to read it. It might answer a lot of questions you have." She patted my hand when I took the note. "I'm only a phone call away if you need me."

I thanked her and walked numbly to my car. I thought about calling Tamsyn, Macey, and my parents all at once because of the breakthrough, but then I realized I didn't even know what that meant or how to explain it in a way that would make sense to anybody but me. I needed to read the book Kerri suggested and see if that helped put thoughts into the right category in my brain. I checked for messages before I put the car in drive. I had three texts, but only one made my heart race.

We're at the hospital. Arya took a ball to the face at school. She's going to need a few stitches but she's okay.

I checked the time. She sent the message fourteen minutes ago. Kerri's office was in the same complex as the hospital but in a different building. I drove to the emergency room, parked, and raced through the doors. "Arya Hayes. She's here for stitches."

"Are you family?" the triage nurse asked.

Without hesitation, I answered yes. "I'm her aunt."

The seconds seemed so slow for her to find Arya's name in the system. "Room twelve," she said and buzzed me through the locked doors.

She's okay, she's okay, I repeated as I quickly walked down the hall until I found her room. I slid the glass door open and peeked in. Tamsyn and Lauren were on one side of Arya holding her hands while a doctor was stitching up her chin. Arya was crying but remained still. Macey was also in the room and turned when she heard the door. She walked over to me and motioned for me to go out into the hallway with her.

"She's getting eight stitches," Macey said.

She touched my arm to console me. I ignored her warmth and tried to stay in the moment because right now it was about family.

"What are you doing here?" I shook my head because it sounded rude. "Wait, I mean were you called in? Or did you just happen to see her name?" So many emotions were tumbling around inside and I tried hard to stay focused. It was hard when Macey was looking at me with such concern. Her hazel eyes were alert as though looking for distressed signs in mine. I pushed my stupid feelings aside.

"I was called in because she was unconscious for a few seconds. She has a small concussion and obviously she's getting stitched up, but she's going to be fine." She pulled me into her arms to console me, and a wave of peace washed over me. It felt right. I pulled away first because now was not the time for any grand gestures or me begging for another chance. I couldn't explain it, but I felt we were going to be okay.

"Thank you for being here for us. I'm sure she calmed down once she recognized you," I said.

"It helped when I introduced her to the plastic surgeon. She's scared, but not terrified like she was about five minutes ago."

I noticed blood on her collar and shoulder. "Is that from Arya?" I asked. My body felt weak. I could take care of animals who were bloody and needed help, but not my family.

She nodded. "Are you good to go in there? Do you have any questions?"

"I'm okay." I squeezed her hand. "Thank you for taking care of her and telling me what's going on. How are Tamsyn and Lauren holding up?" I couldn't imagine Tamsyn being anything but a rock, but Arya was both her strength and her weakness, so I worried about her.

"They are both amazing. You have wonderful friends."

"They're your friends, too. Regardless of whatever happened with us, you're still their friend," I said. I meant that. Everyone respected and liked Macey. Our breakup had nothing to do with them.

She looked uncomfortable for a moment. "We can talk later. Let's see how they're doing."

I followed her back into the room where the doctor was carefully cleaning up Arya's chin and putting a bandage over the stitches. "Hey, peanut. How are you feeling?" I gave Tamsyn and Lauren quick hugs before turning my attention back to the patient. I couldn't get close enough to hug her but gave her knee a squeeze. "You're so brave."

"She's an excellent patient," the doctor said.

After Tamsyn and Lauren thanked him profusely, he promised to get care instructions and discharge papers as soon as possible. Macey followed him out.

Tamsyn nodded in the direction of the door. "She was great."

I shrugged and waved her off. "She said Arya was a good patient. Let's get this little bug home. I can pick up some easy food for dinner tonight. Any suggestions?" I pointed to Arya's chin. "Can she open her mouth?"

"We'll probably just do something easy like a smoothie and maybe a Gogurt. How does that sound?"

Arya reached her arms out and Lauren scooped her up. I hadn't realized how big she'd gotten until I saw her wrapped around Lauren. She was half her size.

"What happened?" I asked.

Tamsyn answered. "Some older kids were hitting a baseball around at recess and Arya got in the way." She moved so that Lauren and Arya could have her chair.

"Well, Macey said she will be just fine," I said.

"We're so happy she was in the hospital today. She was down here in a flash with a plastic surgeon. She wouldn't let the ER doctor do the sutures." Tamsyn gently pushed Arya's hair away from her face.

Macey returned with a stack of papers. "The papers on top are instructions for how to take care of the sutures. Try to keep them dry for twenty-four to forty-eight hours." She leaned down to look at Arya. "Sorry, kiddo. That means no swimming until they are healed."

"How many weeks until it's healed?" Lauren asked.

"Oh, they'll only be in for about four or five days. If you want, I can swing by this weekend and take a look at them." She lowered her voice so only Tamsyn and I could hear her. "I can take them out if she's healed."

"That would be amazing. Wouldn't you like that more, Arya? Aunt Macey can come to the house and take them out so we don't have to come back here," Tamsyn said. Arya nodded.

"And these are the release papers. You are free to go," Macey said.

Tamsyn gathered Macey in a bear hug and kissed her cheek. "Thank you for taking care of our baby. Obviously, we'll be home all weekend, so give me a call when you have a free moment."

"You're welcome. I'll call you," Macey said.

When she turned to me, I felt tiny jolts of electricity in the three feet that separated us. Little pings of excitement bounced under my skin. I smiled softly at her. "Thanks for taking care of them so quickly."

"No problem. Will you be there this weekend, too?" she asked.

I didn't know what to say. I was always invited, but did she want me there or no? Tamsyn's arm around my shoulders jump-started my brain. I leaned into her.

"I can be. If it's okay with everyone."

"You're always invited. If you have time. I know things are super busy in your world right now," Tamsyn said.

She was trying to bait Macey and it worked.

"Oh, how's it going? Is Healing Paws still going to open on time?" She shook her head. "Wait. You all have somewhere better to be than here. Take Arya home and we can catch up this weekend," she said.

"Yes, let's get out of here. I've spent way too much time in this place," I said. I was only half-joking, but we quickly scooted out of the hospital. "I'll pick up dinner and meet you at the house."

❖

I put the tray of smoothies on Tamsyn's counter and watched my parents speed waltz around the room to Katy Perry's latest song blasting through the Bluetooth speakers. I loved that they still danced. Tamsyn and Arya were slowly swaying in one spot.

"She has to stay awake until nine because of her concussion," Tamsyn said.

"How are you doing, peanut?" I asked.

Arya reached out and I scooped her up.

"Want to see what smoothies I got us?" I felt her nod on my shoulder. She picked the strawberry and banana one. I sat on the chair with her on my lap and we watched my parents playfully twirl around the room. "How long have they been doing this?"

She held up two fingers.

"Two minutes?" I asked.

"Two songs," Arya said.

Her chin was swollen under the large bandage that covered the stitches. She'd have a bruise for a few weeks, but she was the kind of kid who didn't care. "You know what? They're pretty good."

She nodded and leaned against me. I gave her a quick squeeze and pointed to her parents, who were now dancing with mine. Arya's eyes were wide as she watched the couples in front of us dance and sing to her. She wasn't going to fall asleep any time soon.

"You up for a duet?"

Tamsyn crooked her finger at me and queued a Kelly Clarkson song. Lauren switched places with me. I grabbed the television remote as my microphone, ready to sing and dance my heart out. I had a lot of stress I needed to shake loose, but ultimately, I wanted Arya to have a good time and stay alert.

"Arya, you're the judge. You get to pick who sings this song the best," Tamsyn said.

"Remember who got you a delicious treat tonight," I yelled before slipping into my star persona. Tamsyn and I belted out the lyrics, taking turns with the chorus. It was awful but it was working. Arya was still engaged and even smiled. After the third song, I was exhausted and needed a break. I waved off the offer for more singing and headed for the kitchen for a cold drink. When the doorbell rang, I yelled that I would answer it since I was the closest to the door.

"I hope you don't mind me stopping by. I wanted to see how Arya's doing," Macey said.

I wanted to rub my fingers on her forehead to make her pronounced worry lines on her forehead disappear. I leaned against the doorjamb for strength. I wasn't expecting to see her twice in a day. "It's good to see you." Remembering my manners, I rolled my shoulder to the side and invited her in. "The festivities are in the living room. Full disclosure. You might get recruited for really bad karaoke."

She smiled. "That's not going to happen."

I held my hands up. "It's not really up to us. It's whatever the patient wants."

"I know it's getting late, but I also know she needs to stay awake for a bit, so she should still be up."

"Follow the really bad singing. Sounds like my dad's trying to sing 'Johnny B. Goode' and he probably has his audience yawning with boredom. I'm grabbing a glass of water. Would you like one?"

"No, thanks. I just stopped by to check in. I won't be staying long."

A part of me wanted to race after her and stand by her side, watch her every move, and see everyone's reaction when they saw her. But the calmer part of me won, and I took my time pouring my glass of water. Somebody turned the music down and several people spoke at once. I heard my mom's voice first.

"Dr. Burr. It's so good to see you again, but one day I hope it's not because of an emergency."

"Call me Macey. And I certainly hope so, too. I just stopped by to check on Arya. From the looks of it, you all are doing a great job of keeping her awake," Macey said.

I walked into the room because I couldn't stand not being a part of the conversation. All eyes were on Macey and rightfully so. She knelt in front of Arya and was asking her random questions like what was her favorite song we sang tonight, who sang the best, and how Harry the hamster was doing. Arya answered each question easily. Her sentences were short, but she was very aware of her surroundings.

"You're doing great, kiddo," Macey said. She answered a few questions that Tamsyn and Lauren asked and said her good-byes.

"Why don't you stay for a bit?" Lauren asked.

"I can't. I only wanted to check on Arya on my way home. Thank you for the invitation but I really need to get going. I still have work to do."

Tamsyn and I walked her out.

"Thank you, Macey," Tamsyn said.

I remained silent because this wasn't about me. I gave her a soft smile and nodded. She knew I was appreciative.

"Of course. I was on my way home and she's been on my mind. Good night."

We watched Macey walk to her car and waved when she drove away.

"That was really nice of her," Tamsyn said. She linked her arm with mine. "I still think there's something there worth pursuing after the dust settles."

After everything we'd been through and the progress I was making, I hoped so, too.

Chapter Eighteen

Healing Paws was ready for business. I had a few minor things left to do, but in a week, the doors would open and one of the scariest and most exciting chapters in my life would begin. I had so much support from my friends and the community that I decided to go all out for Tricks-for-Treats. The hay bales were in place, but I needed color and my goal was to find fun, festive, fall decorations to make the opening warm and cozy. I was one of the first customers at the farmer's market and scored front row parking. My list included corn stalks, flowers, pumpkins, and anything fall related.

Tamsyn, Lauren, and Arya volunteered to bake dog treats in the shape of bones, and Mom offered to bake salmon cat treats in the shape of fish. Yara and Tiffany were putting together small bags of soft treats for the senior pets, and I was in charge of picking up leafy vegetables in case somebody brought their rodent pet in. It wasn't a huge responsibility and I was thankful. Arya explained to me several times that Harry the hamster liked celery and spinach leaves, but he didn't like iceberg lettuce so I shouldn't get that.

I felt so good about Healing Paws. It was ready to go. Construction finished early, the business passed inspection, and now I was playing the waiting game.

"How much are your pumpkins?" I asked the closest vendor to my van.

"Five for the small ones, eight for the large ones."

The vendor and a young teen were still setting up their booth.

"How many do you have?"

"We have a mix of about twenty. We also have squash, tomatoes, corn, and flowers," he said.

Well, this was going to be an easy trip. "I'll take all the pumpkins as long as you can deliver them to that van over there." I pointed to the bright yellow conversion van that was impossible to miss. Healing Paws Home Healthcare, our phone number, and very adorable cartoon pets were proudly displayed in vinyl across the side.

"No problem," he said.

I paid them and unlocked the van for them to load up. I still had shopping to do. I was going to make my grand opening the best it could be without it being obnoxious. I knew I was going overboard, but it was my way to push Macey from my mind. Not only did I miss her when she took out Arya's stitches because of timing, but she never reached out. I'd hoped we were going to survive, but since she never made the effort, it didn't make sense to keep hoping for something that wasn't there. The world's slowest breakup still hurt.

I fell in love with pink and purple asters a few booths down and filled up the wagon with four beautiful bushy pots. They were animal-friendly in case any of my patients decided to nibble on them and offered bright pops of color in the rather sterile environment in the waiting room. I needed to pick up a large order of framed animal posters from our local hobby store and assemble wire shelves for the dog and cat food we sold. I was in the home stretch, and it was exciting but scary. I stopped wheeling the cart when my mom called.

"How's it going?" she asked.

"It not even eight o'clock and I'm done shopping," I said. I was pleased with what I found and was mentally picturing everything in the clinic until a flash of long, blond, curly hair distracted me. I must've gasped because my mother homed in on it.

"What's wrong?" she asked.

I stumbled a bit. "Oh, uh. Nothing. Nothing's wrong. Listen, Mom. I have to go, but I'll call you when I get to Healing Paws. You can see all the stuff I bought and help me arrange it." I said good-bye and slipped my phone into my back pocket.

My wagon was too full for a quick getaway. Macey was there with a tall, gorgeous brunette who threw her head back when she laughed. She was definitely in Macey's personal space and Macey didn't seem to mind. That explained why she never texted or called me the last several weeks. She had moved on. I awkwardly turned the wagon and made a beeline for the van. Of all the luck. Why was she here? She only took weekends off when it was important. What was so important about the hot, leggy brunette or this weekend? I looked down at my navy blue T-shirt, paint-splattered jeans, and sneakers, instantly regretting dressing so casually. I expected to see nobody I knew because I was going to get dirty cleaning the office this afternoon. I didn't care how I looked when I left my house at six thirty.

I almost got away. I opened the side door and stared at the mountain of pumpkins. My flowers would get crushed if I put them back here and made a hard stop.

"Nice pumpkins." The slyness in her voice was unmistakable.

I braced myself and turned around. I wanted to relax because Legs wasn't around but then I remembered what I looked like. "Oh, hey. What are you doing here?"

"Admiring your pumpkins," she said.

I gave her a polite smile. "I needed a few for my grand opening next weekend. I might even be brave and carve a few. Good exercise for my elbow." In a total dork move, I moved my elbow back and forth to show her I was completely healed even though she already knew that.

"That's a lot of pumpkins to carve. And a few of these are baking pumpkins. Are you saving the brains for baking?"

"Clever joke from a neurologist. Honestly, I thought they were all just plain ole pumpkins. I guess maybe I can roast the seeds?" I flipped my sunglasses onto the top of my head so I could see her better. She looked amazing and my heart hurt just knowing she was so close and I couldn't touch her.

"If you'd like, I can bake something for your grand opening. Little pumpkin pies or pumpkin squares," she said.

"Wouldn't your new friend be upset?" I asked. It was totally high schoolish and immature, but I was notorious for not having a filter around Macey. She looked confused.

"What new friend?" she asked.

I almost said Legs, but I caught myself just in time. "The woman you were just with. Won't she care if you're baking something for me?"

She put her hands on her hips. "You could've said hello if you saw me."

I held my sneer in check. "You looked busy and I didn't want to interrupt. Plus, I'm super busy, too, and I have to get these back to the clinic. I just have a lot to do." I was rambling but I didn't know what she wanted from me.

"Do you need any help?" she asked.

I opened the passenger door and shoved the asters on the floorboard. "No, thank you. I think I'm good."

She reached for my hand.

I immediately looked around for Legs.

"Would you please slow down? I get that you have things to do, but we haven't talked and I feel like we need to, you know?"

She looked vulnerable and very kissable. I relaxed my shoulders and gently pulled my hand away. She frowned. "I'm sorry I missed you at Tamsyn's when I took Arya's stitches out, but I was on call, and sure enough, the one time I didn't want to be working, I had to go in. I was only at Tamsyn's for a few minutes," she said.

I knew that was true because five minutes after I got the secret text from Tamsyn, she sent me another one to tell me Macey got called away. "That was a bummer." I visibly tensed when I saw

Legs walking up behind Macey carrying two doughnuts. How cute. Macey turned at my reaction.

"Hey, you found me. Alyssa, this is Sawyer." She turned back to me with a small smile perched on her lips. "Sawyer, this is my sister-in-law, Alyssa."

Fuck off. She did that on purpose. "Hi, nice to meet you." I tried to gradually relax my body so it wasn't obvious to the world that I assumed they were together. "How do you have the weekend off? Is it a special weekend?" I asked.

"It's my brother's birthday. We came down here to find something different and unique for him but ended up finding stuff for ourselves," Macey said.

"He's so difficult to shop for. Instead of the usual shirt or gift card we normally get him, we thought maybe the market would have a cool antique or something repurposed like a funky light or end table that used to be a boat anchor," Alyssa said. She shrugged like she didn't care or didn't have hope that they would find something.

"The lawyer, the accountant, or the store owner? Sounds like the beginning of a bad joke," I said. Nobody laughed.

"Damon, the lawyer. He buys anything he wants so he's hard to shop for," Macey said.

"Well, you can't go wrong with doughnuts," I said. This time I got chuckles from both.

"Nice to meet you, Sawyer. Macey, I'm going to go any-where but here, so text me when you're done," Alyssa said.

Ugh. That meant that everyone knew.

"Will do," Macey said.

They exchanged a look I couldn't identify, and that made me wary. My anxiety was back up to a ten. "So, I guess I'd better get going. I'm sure all these people driving around would kill for this spot."

"Why don't you pick a day, right now, when I can come over and we can gut these gourds and I can bake something for your opening?" she asked. She inspected a few of the smaller pumpkins. "Healing Paws is so important to you, and I want to contribute. I can't bring you any animals to heal, but I can bribe their owners with my baking."

How could she act like the last month didn't bother her? That not talking to me didn't keep her awake at night like it did me? "How come you never reached out to me?"

She took a step back and crossed her arms. "What do you mean? You never texted me."

"But the ball was in your court. I thought since our run-in at the hospital when Arya got hurt, maybe you wanted to get together and talk but I never heard from you." I shrugged like "oh, well" but it hurt.

She touched my arm. She always touched me as though her nearness wasn't enough to get my attention. "I'm sorry, but I was trying to respect your space since you were the one really upset with me. Had I known you would've accepted my calls, I would've reached out sooner."

I knew if I really wanted to work things out with Macey, I needed to decide if I was willing to pursue a future with her. I could either still be mad or start fresh. "Well, okay." I took a deep breath. "If you really want to help with the pumpkins, what day works the best for you? My schedule is obviously open."

"How about Tuesday? I should be able to get out of work at six and be at your place about six thirty?"

"Okay, I'll see you then," I said.

She put her palm on the van. "I really like this. I think it's a great idea and you're going to get a lot of business."

I smiled for the first time in ten minutes. "Thanks. I'll see you soon." I didn't watch her walk away. I needed to get in the car and call Tamsyn.

"Are you awake?" I asked when she finally answered.

"It's Saturday. I've been up since six. Hang on. Let me go into the kitchen and grab a cup of coffee."

I heard her shuffle to the kitchen and clang coffee cups in

the cabinet. "It's almost eight thirty. Why are you just getting coffee?"

"No sports or dance this weekend. We're living it up. Lauren is still in bed. What's going on?"

"I have a van full of pumpkins and flowers, so that was a success. Guess who I ran into at the farmer's market?"

"I'm going to say Macey because you're pretty damn excited," she said.

"Ding, ding, ding. She's coming over this week to help me carve some pumpkins and gut the baking ones so she can bake little pies for my grand opening," I said. I waited for excitement, for any acknowledgment but she yawned again.

"Oh, really?" She was not impressed.

"You're probably tired of hearing all of this." I sighed. It was a lot for anyone, and Tamsyn had been dealing with this part of my life almost daily for months.

"No, I'm sorry. You're right. I'm a bad friend. Tell me what happened."

Tamsyn already knew the breakthrough I made in therapy. She pushed me to reach out to Macey after we didn't meet up when Arya got her stitches out, but I had moved past angry to just embarrassed. I didn't know what I could even say to Macey.

After I told her about running into Macey, she asked, "How do you feel about it?"

"I mean, I'm a little hesitant, but I'm also excited at the possibility of starting over with her. She has to know things are different with me now. And you know she's my dream girl," I joked. It was funny now, but it was a rocky road.

Tamsyn snorted. "Yeah, don't ever tell her that."

"Not after everything that's happened. Okay, I'm home. Go spend time with your family. Kiss them from me. I'm going to pack my place with pumpkins, then head to the clinic," I said. Even though mostly everything was done, I still had so much to do.

"Let me know if you need any help. We're around," she said.

"Next weekend is when I'll need you all the most." I disconnected the call and spent the next fifteen minutes unloading the van.

It was good to see you today.

I was torn between responding immediately and waiting thirty seconds. I compromised and fifteen seconds later, I typed *It was good to see you, too.*

I'll see you Tuesday night at your place.

Okay looking forward to it.

CHAPTER NINETEEN

The first knock startled me, but it was the urgency of the raps tapping on Healing Paws' door that spiked my pulse. It was seven thirty Monday night, and I was hanging posters and organizing the receptionist's desk. The waiting area had to be aesthetically pleasing to both clients and staff, and I was pleased with my décor. I peeked out the window to find Macey holding a box. I quickly unlocked the door.

"What are you doing here?" I asked.

She must have picked up on the alarm in my voice. "I didn't mean to scare you, but you weren't answering your phone."

"What's wrong?" I was extremely curious about the box she was holding very carefully close to her chest. I waved her inside. Her face lit up as she surveyed the waiting room.

"This is beautiful, Sawyer," she said.

"Thank you." I paused for a moment to give her time to soak it all in. It wasn't ready, but it was close enough. "Now, what's in the box?"

She walked to the counter and carefully put the box down. "This might sound like a pickup line, and maybe it is, but I found a box of kittens and knew you would be able to help."

I pushed aside the need to stare at her longer. There were subtle changes in the way she styled her hair, and how her nails were shorter and painted a copper color that complemented her hazel eyes, and how her tan lines that peeked out from the open collar of her shirt were fading.

"Kittens! What the heck?" I folded back the flaps of the box and discovered two sweet, fluffy kittens that couldn't have been more than three weeks old curled up together. "Where did you find these?"

"One of the nurses found them on the side of the hospital. I'm sorry to just barge over here, but I knew you could help," she said.

I scooped the fuzzy black one up and gave it a quick but careful checkup. "Slightly malnourished, but no other glaring problems. Also, male." I handed him to Macey, who immediately tucked him against her chest. Lucky cat, I thought. I picked up the other kitten, a gray ball of fluff who meowed hungrily. "It's a girl," I said with a celebratory tone. "Are you ready to bottle-feed kittens?" At her nod, I said, "follow me."

I mixed some kitten formula and found two bottles. Macey smiled so genuinely at me that I almost kissed her. Instead, I handed her a bottle and showed her how to get the kitten to drink.

"Why isn't he taking it?" she asked.

"You have to be patient. We don't know their history, but obviously something traumatic happened or else they would still be with their mother and not abandoned by the side of the hospital. Why don't you take her, and I'll figure out how to get this little bug to feed?" Our fingers got entangled during the swap, and a warmth spread through me as I remembered the magic her hands created on my body.

"This is so adorable," she said.

I got the boy to take the small nipple and watched as his little claws flexed around my fingers. This part of my job never got old. The pure joy and trust that animals gave us. "How do you feel about having a few kittens around your house?"

She pursed her lips and finally shook her head. "It wouldn't be fair. Why don't you keep them here as office kitties? I mean,

I'm more than willing to have them come over for sleepovers during long weekends, but I don't feel like I could give them the time or the love."

I chuckled. It was obvious she never had a pet before. She hadn't experienced the need to race home and spend time snuggling and playing. "Your idea has merit. Office cats are always a hit. Most of the time they manage to ease some stress, but sometimes they create it. If they stay here, I'll have to put a note on the door so that they aren't chased by wound-up doggos."

"Did Oliver Strong have an office pet?"

I grumbled. "Yes, but he hated every second of their existence. He was always worried they would knock over things or get in the way, but he didn't realize that's the fun part of having them. Office cats don't give a crap." I looked at the two kittens. I had no idea what their personalities would be like, but now that I had my own business, I could always run home and check on them. When they were old enough, I could do trial runs here at the office. "Look at me thinking of keeping them." I touched their silky ears and made little cooing noises.

"It's nice to see you at work. You're very good."

I laughed. "Come on. They are kittens. And relatively healthy ones. This isn't really me in my element, but I'm glad you're here." The space suddenly felt very small.

"I was at a complete loss of what to do. I full-on panicked," Macey said.

"I doubt that. You're a levelheaded doctor. And these are tiny little bodies. They need food, warmth, and love."

She stroked the male's head. "You called him bug. I think that should be his name. Bug. Just a cute little bug."

"Just wait until we have to make them go to the bathroom," I said. She looked horrified. I couldn't help but smile. She dealt with the brain and had seen some awful injuries, and she was standing in front of me nervous to treat a small animal.

"It's okay. I've got this. They aren't ready yet. Why don't we let them nap for a bit and I'll show you the place. If you want," I said.

"I thought you'd never ask," she said.

Macey was my first tour with somebody who wasn't family or staff. My heart was bursting with pride and happiness because she was here with me after everything we'd been through. We weren't where I wanted us to be, but this was a step in the right direction.

"A trip to the vet is nerve-wracking for both patient and owner." I stopped because I sounded like a commercial. "I hope that it's not too clinical. I want it to be warm and inviting, but it has to be able to stand up for the next five or so years." Oliver's décor was stuck in the nineties.

"I love everything about this place. The playdate area is adorable, the waiting room is comfortable, and your services are amazing. I can't imagine it not being an instant success. Do you have appointments already?"

"The first two weeks are already full." I smirked because so many customers from Oliver Strong called for appointments either excited to transition to me or curious about my place.

She clutched my hand. "You have to be so proud."

"All of this is because I got in a car wreck." My life had changed so much in six months. Most of it was good, but it took an emotional toll on me. Physically, I healed fine with a few scars, but mentally I was in a different head space. Therapy was something I never considered, but what a difference it had made. I found out so much about myself in the sessions with Kerri—and not just about my dream world. I planned on continuing therapy once a week. Starting a new business was a different kind of stress and I wasn't too proud to admit I needed her help.

"This is your office? I can see a few cat beds here by the window and a litter box over there in the closet. I think Bug and his sister would love it here. What should we call her? She's such a delicate little lady," Macey said.

I learned that coincidences shouldn't be ignored. I waited

until Macey made the connection. Her reaction didn't disappoint. Her eyes widened and her mouth fell open.

"Well. I wasn't expecting that, but it seems fitting," she said.

Macey carefully plucked the gray kitten away from Bug's clutches and held her against her chest. I watched how gentle she was with her and knew one or both kittens would end up living at her place. Or mine. They had already bonded, so I didn't want to break that up.

"Lady and Bug." I shrugged as though they were just names for pets when we both knew those were anything but random. I pictured Tamsyn yelling at me for keeping Ladybug Junction alive, but without it, I would've never pursued Macey or looked for signs that she was interested in me. "They will have to be fed one more time tonight, and I don't plan on staying here all night. I guess I'll take them home."

"I'm so sorry. I didn't know what else to do." Macey biting her bottom lip looking worried made me clear my throat and find a reason to get away from her. She was too close and I was too vulnerable.

"You did the right thing. I'm going to grab a few things here, and then take these fluffernutters back to my place." The silent invitation hung in the air. I wanted her to want to come over. Had I asked, she would have said yes, but then I would have wondered if guilt played a part.

"Do you mind if I come over? I can help do another feeding and maybe you can show me how to make them go to the bathroom."

I laughed as she tried to keep her voice even, but her words faltered. "You're a doctor. You've seen people at their worst. Blood, guts, brains, and yet you're frightened by a kitten's poo," I said. I pulled a small litterbox off the shelf and added litter. "You changed your nieces' and nephews' diapers, right?"

"Yeah, but that was after the fact."

I handed her a small bag of supplies. "Here, take this and I'll grab the babies. It'll be fun to show you something you can add to your résumé. Skills include healing people with brain injuries, helping patients who have had strokes or seizures, and making kittens go to the bathroom. You're bound to get a job anywhere."

She put her hand on my arm. Hearing her laugh was the best sound. It was light and weaved its way into my body and squeezed something inside my chest. Even though we agreed to get together tomorrow and I was mentally preparing myself for hours with her, tonight was a nice surprise. For once, I was helping her. I got to step in and save the day.

"Let me shut off the lights and lock up," I said.

I was pumped as I drove home with kittens beside me and Macey in her coupe behind me. The night didn't go as I expected, but I was more than happy at the way it turned out. Not only was I spending alone time with Macey, but she finally got to see me in my element. Lady lifted her tiny head and looked up at me before she meowed. "It's okay, baby. We're going to be home soon." By the time I pulled up in my driveway, both kittens were alert and very vocal.

"How'd they do on the drive over?" Macey asked. She looked in the box and smiled as they looked up at her and meowed louder.

"Are they hungry?" she asked.

"They probably need everything. To go to the bathroom, eat some more, and curl up against us. Are you ready?" At Macey's nod, I unlocked my door and set them up inside my bathroom. I grabbed a soft hypoallergenic baby wipe, flipped Bug on his back, and massaged his belly and groin until he relieved himself.

"That's it?" Macey asked.

"That's it," I said. I handed her a wipe and she did the same thing with Lady and produced the exact same results. "And we shouldn't have to do this much longer. By the end of the week or early next, they should feel comfortable going with the litterbox."

"Because they're bigger?" she asked.

"Because we're going to introduce them to wet food after a few days. They're able to walk around and stay alert. Usually that's a good sign they are healthy and growing." I rubbed my thumb over Lady's tiny head. "I wonder where they came from?"

"I wish I knew. One of the nurses went outside on break and came back in with kittens. I mean, if you're going to dump animals, a hospital isn't a bad place," Macey said.

We were shoulder to shoulder sitting on the bathroom floor, watching them mewling and learning their new space. I was ready for pets, and cats were the obvious choice. They could keep each other company while I worked, and once they were old enough, they could, if their personalities allowed it, come to work and be office cats.

"I never realized how playful kittens are," Macey said. She quickly drew back her hand. "Or how pointy their tiny nails are."

"Like the edges of razor blades. I'll have tiny marks all over me until they figure out not to use them on the hand that feeds them."

"Well, they are super sweet and I don't think they're doing it on purpose."

Once Bug found the tiny round bed I brought from supply shelves, it was lights out for him. It took Lady a little bit of time to find him, but once she did, she snuggled up beside him. Macey pulled out her phone and took several photos of them wrapped up together.

"The staff will be excited to see how well they are adjusting. I told them my girlfriend is a veterinarian and they handed them to me and abandoned me," she said.

I froze. It was the first time she called me her girlfriend. We hadn't even talked about our relationship or what direction we were headed in. I was confused. "We should probably talk about that," I said.

"I think so, too. The babies look like they're going to nap for a bit and we have time before their next meal. How about we leave them here and go downstairs and talk?"

I shrugged out of my paint shirt and placed it next to them so when they woke they would smell something familiar. I closed the door and pulled a clean T-shirt from my dresser and met Macey downstairs. "I feel like I need to tell you about my therapy and the things Kerri and I uncovered during our sessions."

"Are you still seeing her?" Macey asked.

I handed her a glass of ice water and sat down at the dining room table opposite her. This was a better place to have a serious conversation. It would be too easy to slip into sex if we were on the couch. "I am. With the new business gearing up, my stress level is high and it's a different kind than I had before. Thank you for recommending her to me. She's fantastic."

"She's one of the best. I'm happy to hear she was able to help you," Macey said.

"She helped me through a lot of dream world versus reality, but the big breakthrough I had was when I figured out that the Macey from Ladybug Junction was really a person who had all the qualities I wanted." Macey cocked her head and pursed her lips while processing that information. I explained further. "At the very beginning of therapy, Kerri asked me to write down things I admired about dream Macey. I said things like carefree, ambitious, loyal to herself and her family. Then several months later she asked me to write down things I wanted to change about myself." I squeezed Macey's hand. "The lists were almost identical. When I was in my coma, my brain needed to tuck those qualities somewhere and picked you." I was excited to share my big breakthrough with her, but started doubting everything while she sat there in silence. It never occurred to me that maybe she wouldn't believe me.

"I can tell you've made a breakthrough. I'm just so sorry that I added time to your healing process. I have learned so much just from your experience. I no longer sit with my patients when I'm on personal calls for fear that my words and conversations might seep into their unconscious thoughts. It was so unfair of me to be a jerk about that. I'm a neurologist. I should have been more aware." She balled her hands into fists out of self-anger.

I held her hands. "I'm not upset at you. I'm just happy it's all clear to me now. I know who you are. Dr. Macey Burr, sexy, sweet, passionate neurologist who hates carnivals, loves to sing, works long hours, and is afraid to have a pet because she might neglect them. Thank you for not dismissing me right away and for giving us a second chance. Relationships are hard and I'm willing to do what it takes to figure out what we have. I don't want to walk away from this." I knew she had feelings for me because why would she call me her girlfriend if she didn't believe we could get past this?

"Thank you for forgiving me. You're right. Relationships are hard and you're worth fighting for. I want us to get back on track. I miss you and I don't want to miss out on more milestones in your life," she said.

"I mean, sure, opening up my own business is big and all, but kittens are a pretty big commitment. Are you sure you're up for that?"

"They're really cute," she said.

Our playful banter made my heart swell. She was in. She wanted this relationship as much as I did. Macey of Ladybug Junction was gone. Honestly, the Macey sitting in front of me, holding my hand from across the table, was my dream girl.

CHAPTER TWENTY

I had twenty pumpkins scrubbed clean on my kitchen floor and on the table. When Macey texted that she was on her way, I told her the front door was unlocked.

"Hello? I'm here."

My body tingled and I felt my pulse kick-start at her voice. "I'm in the kitchen," I yelled.

"Looks like you're getting mugged by a gang of pumpkins. Do you need saving?" she asked. She dropped her purse on the counter and threw her hair back in a ponytail. I loved watching her do simple things. She was graceful and confident.

"Always. You look great. And I'd hug you, but there are way too many gourds between me and you. I'll have to carve my way to you. Also, please tell me you brought clothes to wear because I don't want you to get orange guts all over your silk blouse and pants."

"I forgot, but I'm a pro at not getting dirty in dirty situations," she said.

I was already in yoga pants and an old painting T-shirt. "Absolutely not. Let me find a path out of this mob and I'll get you something you can wear. Pumpkins are messy." I wanted to kiss her anyway.

"Where are the babies?" she asked, looking around the room for any signs of them.

I pointed upstairs as I jumped from bare spot to bare spot until I hopped right in front of her. She put her arms out to steady me. "Hello," I said.

She gathered my T-shirt in her fist and pulled me closer. "Hi." Her lips were on mine in less than a second. I wanted to float away but she was holding me against her body. I wasn't complaining.

"Let's get you out of these clothes." I wiggled my eyebrows playfully. "And say hello to the babies. I just fed them, so they might be sleeping. We can bring them down here if you want." At her nod, I linked our fingers and led her to my room. Last night, she stayed over until after midnight. We talked about our relationship, what we wanted, what we expected, and ended the night with a sweet kiss and a new beginning. I rummaged through my dresser for something for her to wear while she peeked in on the kittens.

"They're still sleeping," she whispered and put her finger up to her lips.

"Why don't you bring them down after you change? That way they can be with us, and when they're awake, we can play with them between gutting the gourds." I handed her the clothes, kissed her, and closed the door behind me. I wanted to stay and help her undress and eventually dress, but I had too many things on my mind and couldn't relax. I was nervous about the VIP Tricks-for-Treats event Sunday and the grand opening Monday. I ordered a pizza and made a workable path through the pumpkins while I waited for her to join me.

"I can't believe how adorable they are. I showed everyone at work how well they did last night and today," Macey said.

She had the kittens in their bed and carefully put them in the dining room away from the bright lights. I knew it was a matter of time before she raced over here after work every day just to play with them. She asked me to send her photos throughout the day. She was hooked and didn't even know it.

"They did really well." I was surprised at how well they took to us. They weren't scared once they realized we were feeding them and keeping them safe. "So, are you ready to carve or just here for the guts?"

She put her arms around my waist and leaned back to look at me. "Don't be mad, but I have more pumpkins in the car. With the exception of the little pumpkins over there, the rest are worthless to me. For baking, I mean. These are great for decorations and carving a few -o-lanterns, but I needed the good flesh."

I looked around my kitchen at the fifteen basketball-sized pumpkins. "It's sad that I know nothing about pumpkins or how pies are made. I thought you used the pulp of these."

"Good news. Homemade roasted pumpkin seeds are delicious, and we can use the seeds from any of those pumpkins," Macey said. She pointed to the ones I just cleaned for the last hour. "And we can put whatever spices we want on them," she said.

I groaned. "How do I know so little about pumpkins?"

"You don't bake, and I do. Let's organize the pumpkins, grab the ones from my car, and get to work. Moping isn't going to get them done any faster." She kissed my pouting lips until I smiled.

We organized them by shape and quality. I was the muscle of Operation Pumpkin. She put me to work cutting and gutting the baking ones. Then I scooped out the guts of the ones we agreed to carve faces in. By nine, I was exhausted, but Lady and Bug needed the bottle.

"Why don't you just stay the night and I'll make sure you don't oversleep. What time is your first appointment?" I asked.

"I have rounds at eight thirty. I can't be late."

I pulled her in my arms. "Okay, instead, why don't you go home and get some rest? You've been at it all day, and this week is only going to get busier. We can load up what you want to cook at your place because your kitchen is dynamite and my kitchen is like outdoor cooking with one hot plate."

"We can roast the seeds here. They're pretty tough and can handle a lopsided environment like your oven," she said.

"It's practically brand new. I look at it like a bonus for when I sell the place. Oven rarely used."

"Are you moving?" she asked.

I laughed. "Not yet, but someday. This isn't really a forever home. If the business takes off, then maybe I can upgrade in a few years." Talking about the future made me nervous, and I didn't want bad luck. I pointed at the buckets full of pumpkin flesh, cut and ready to bake. "Those are really heavy. Are you going to be able to carry them into your house?" With her eight-burner stovetop and two ovens, baking there would be a cinch.

"I'm stronger than I look. I'm more worried about fitting all of this in my fridge since I can't get started on baking until tomorrow night," she said.

I stopped and pulled her into a hug. "Thank you for wanting to help make my grand opening wonderful." I held her close to me, cherishing her warmth and acceptance. We'd been though a lot the last few months.

She leaned back and touched my face. "You're welcome. I know it's going to be amazing."

I didn't want to let her go, but just because I didn't have a set schedule in place yet didn't mean I could keep her from hers.

"Can we feed the babies first?" she asked.

I playfully frowned. "Did you come over just to feed and play with my p—"

She put her hand over my mouth. "Don't you dare soil those beautiful babies with crass language."

My laugh was garbled under her fingers. I pulled back. "It's not crass. It's the truth. You're using me to get to them, aren't you?" We both knew that was far from the truth, but she played along.

"Why else would I be here, elbow deep in pumpkin pulp if not to get closer to those fur babies?"

"Uh, maybe because I'm awesome and we're great together?"

She pretended to ponder that statement. "Yeah, well, maybe that, too."

"Let's get bottles ready."

She gave a little jump for joy and a quiet squeal of excitement. I smiled at her enthusiasm. This was the same woman who had nerves of steel during emergencies and had the utmost patience with her patients. I pulled out two tiny bottles and heated them up in a bowl of warm water. Once the temperature was right, I gave her one and we scooped up the babies and sat on the couch to feed them.

"They are so adorable," she said.

She had Bug, who knew what the bottle was and mewled loudly whenever he saw it. He stretched his toes out and grabbed anything he could to latch onto and eat as much as he could as fast as he could.

"We should've named him Hog or Hoss," I said. Lady was different. She was trusting and not as frenzied during feeding time. "Hello, sweet girl. Are you hungry? Would you like some milk?" I didn't want to tell Macey that they were notorious for conking out and, ten minutes later, ready to play. If I told her that, she'd never leave and never get any sleep. After she left, I would take them back upstairs until they were ready to explore. Right now, small, familiar spaces were ideal to keep them feeling safe.

"He's milk-drunk," Macey said. She placed him on her chest and petted him softly until he fell asleep.

"Lady is a lady. She's so careful and dainty. No milk mustaches here," I said. When she finally finished, I put her on my chest until she fell asleep, too. "Okay, now is the time to make a break for it." I gently placed Lady next to Bug in their bed. "Let's get you loaded up so you can get to bed at a decent time."

It was ten by the time we cleaned up and had the pumpkins loaded in her car. I had a large bowl of seeds that we would roast later in the week. I gave her another hug.

"Text me when you get home. I need to check on the kittens." She kissed me hard, and when she tried to pull away, I grabbed her. "Don't kiss me like that and then leave."

"It'll keep. It always does," she said.

I watched her drive away, lost in my own thoughts until I remembered two kittens inside who were probably ready to crawl out of their bed and get into trouble somewhere.

❖

"Who are these babies?"

Yara scooped up Bug and nuzzled his head.

"Some asshole dumped these two at the hospital and Macey brought them over the other night," I said. It was Friday afternoon. I was tired, but I was so pumped for the opening. Yara was just as excited for Healing Paws as I was and volunteered to help with the finishing touches. At this point, I was dusting and sweeping an already clean waiting room. This morning we hung pet motivational canvas prints in the examination rooms, filled the drawers with necessary supplies, and checked the portable equipment to ensure it was all working properly.

"What are you going to do with them?" she asked.

"Hopefully, they'll be office cats, but right now, they are mine and Macey's." It felt good including Macey because they were the first "ours." We didn't pick them out or anything, but we made a commitment the other night not just between us, but with them. "The black one is Bug and the gray one is Lady."

"They're so cute. How old? Four weeks?" she asked.

"That's what I'm thinking. I'll start them on wet food this week. Big Boy Bug is always hungry. He'd eat ten times a day if I offered."

Yara sat on the floor next to their bed. "Thank you for hiring me. I'm very excited about this place."

She agreed to be office manager and lead technician. I wasn't sure if that was a real job title, but we both understood the responsibilities. She was in charge of two technicians. Eventually, we'd hire a receptionist, but in the meantime, my mom wanted to help. I was nervous with only one other veterinarian on staff, but I was looking to expand and had several résumés to review. I wanted to see how the first month went. Judging by the calendar, all our checkup and non-emergency appointments were almost full for November. We got a lot of calls in the last few days.

"Thank you for wanting to go on this journey with me," I said. I valued Yara and appreciated her leap to do this with me.

Oliver had a meltdown when she quit. Yara gave two weeks' notice, but he was so nasty she packed up her things after one day. I felt a little guilty, but then I remembered he wasn't a great boss and I was going to try to be everything he wasn't.

"Every single person at Oliver Strong wants to come here, but I'm really happy with who we hired," Yara said.

While I liked the staff there, I didn't like how easily manipulated they were. I wanted a fresh start. Yara had found a recent graduate and a technician with ten years' experience who was returning to the workforce after raising three children.

"It's a good vibe. Even Edward seems cool," she said.

Edward was a veterinarian in our area who came highly recommended by one of my colleagues from the conference. I'd met Edward at a few local events over the years, so when I found out he was looking for something different, I reached out. It was a good fit.

Yara and I sat in companionable silence playing with the kittens until they curled up to nap again. "That's my cue. Let's get out of here. I'll see you Sunday."

"I'll bring something."

"Thanks," I said. I grabbed the babies and headed home. Tonight would be my last night of relaxation before the welcome chaos began. I wanted to stop by and see Tamsyn, but it was early, and I knew better than to stop by with kittens. Arya would've lost her mind and pestered Tamsyn and Lauren for kittens until they caved. I pulled up in my driveway, surprised to see Macey's car already parked. She exited her car when I hit the garage door opener. I rolled down my window. "What a nice surprise! What are you doing here"—I quickly checked the clock—"at three thirty on a Friday afternoon?"

"I know you're dealing with a lot, plus I wanted to bring over treats for your approval," she said.

How did I get so lucky? She was wearing black leggings, ankle boots, an Emory T-shirt, and an unbuttoned buffalo check flannel shirt with the sleeves rolled up. Her hair was pulled up in a high ponytail and she was wearing very little makeup. She was beautiful and she was mine.

"It's seventy-two degrees. Aren't you wearing too many clothes?" I teased her.

"I've been baking pumpkin things all week. I need to feel like it's fall outside. This is the best I can do," she said.

"You look amazing. Let's go in." I pulled into the garage and parked.

She thrust the box she was holding at me when I slid out of the car and quickly opened the back door. "Where are my babies? Hello, sweet Bugaboo and Ladyboo." She plucked both kittens from their bed and nuzzled them gently.

"It's not even been a week and I've been replaced." I playfully groaned, but secretly I was thrilled at how well she took to them.

"Don't listen to your other mommy. She's got a lot going on. I'm here to rescue you." She turned to me. "Is it feeding time?"

"Not for a few hours. It's potty time," I said.

She quickly handed them back to me. "You go help them do that, and I'm going to unload my car."

What was she unloading? I was back in ten minutes and surprised to see an overnight bag on the couch. She was staying the night. Adrenaline pushed quickly through my veins as I thought about what that meant. Alone time with Macey was always very hot and passionate.

"You have been so busy with the kittens and Healing Paws

that tonight you're going to get a solid eight hours of sleep and I'm going to take care of the babies."

"You don't have to do that. I rarely get that much sleep as it is."

Her voice lowered. "Do you not want me to stay?"

I cupped her face. "Of course I do. But you're busier than I am."

"But not nearly as stressed. You have me all weekend, if you want."

I nodded. "I want, I want."

"Good. Now let's do a taste testing of the things I baked and you tell me if they're good enough for the grand opening." She kissed me swiftly and stared at my lips for several seconds before looking directly into my eyes. "You can tell me exactly what you like and what you don't like."

Goose bumps raced along my skin and I stifled a shiver. Tonight just got way more interesting.

CHAPTER TWENTY-ONE

"Macey, these are incredible. How? When did you have time?" I popped another cinnamon pumpkin mini muffin into my mouth and moaned my appreciation. The giant smile on her face at my approval made my insides turn to mush. I reached for a pumpkin and cream cheese bar. "Oh my God. These are even better." I waited until I was done chewing. "Seriously, when did you have time to bake all of these?" Besides the muffins and bars, she had peanut butter pumpkin cookies, pumpkin cheesecake, and tiny loaves of pumpkin bread.

"I didn't have any cases that needed extra attention. And I love baking. All of this was easy," she said.

I knew it took time, and that was the one thing she didn't have. My shoulders dropped at the weight of knowing she did this for me. I couldn't believe I was tearing up. "Thank you."

"Call it a labor of love."

I couldn't disguise my surprise. It was a popular saying and people said it all the time, but having tiptoed around this relationship, every word meant something.

She caught herself before I had a complete internal emotional meltdown. "You know what I mean. This wasn't hard at all. I just threw ingredients together and let the oven do its magic." She laughed nervously and busied herself rinsing off the forks we used and washing her hands for a very long time.

I stood in the middle of the kitchen, leaning on the island that separated us, and watched her. We'd been through a lot in such a short time. I knew couples who moved in together after knowing each other only two weeks. Macey could have thrown our relationship away, saying I was too confused and not worthy of a second and even third chance. She was the real deal. She was smart, sexy, responsible, empathetic, passionate, beautiful, and patient. God, was she patient. My dream girl was standing in my kitchen, ten feet away. I could have told her how nice it was to have her here supporting me as I embarked on this new professional journey. I could have mentioned all the reasons she was important to me or how much my friends and family reminded me not to fuck things up with her. Instead, I said what I knew to be undeniably true in my heart.

"I love you, Macey," I said.

The sound of running water splashing in the porcelain sink was the only noise in the otherwise silent kitchen. She was unbelievably still with her back to me. I knew she heard me. Every second she didn't turn around or acknowledge what I said felt like a hundred-pound weight added to the stress on my heart. I felt heavy yet liberated with the truth out in the open. I blew out a deep breath. "Maybe I shouldn't have said that yet, but I mean it." Still no movement. I closed the box of treats and put it in the refrigerator. Nothing. "I'm going to go upstairs and check on the kittens." I needed to give her space to process my words and either come up to me or grab her bag and race home.

I slid to the bathroom floor and gently picked up both kittens and placed them on my lap. Bug blinked at me and awkwardly and sleepily climbed up my shirt to get to my shoulder. His favorite place to sleep was in the crook of my neck and my shoulder surrounded by my hair. "Ow. Ow." I winced with each step, but I loved every second. Lady got as far as my chest and dropped on my not-so-ample cleavage. I held her in place with my hand. I was trapped here and one hundred percent okay. Macey and

I both needed space. "I don't regret it, babies. She needed to know." Bug flexed his jellybean toes and purred contently. It was the first time I'd heard the tiny rumble in his chest.

I wasn't surprised when the door opened. I smiled when Macey sat beside me.

"You have a Bug in your hair," she said.

"This is the only time I'll be okay with those words," I said.

"Speaking of words, those were some pretty powerful words you dropped in the kitchen."

My anxiety was ramping up as I thought about backpedaling, but I wanted her to know. And if that changed the direction of our relationship, at least I could say I gave it my all. "I know. Now probably wasn't the best time, but it's what I felt."

She gingerly plucked Lady off my chest and put her on her lap. She held my hand. "It was lovely and unexpected. I'm not easily surprised, but you managed."

"You're lucky Bug has me in a power hold because I can't move my head to look at you or tell you all the reasons why I do."

She placed Lady gently in her bed and moved so that she straddled my outstretched legs. "So, you can't move, huh?"

"I'm held here in a death grip. Send help?" I was hoping my light playfulness eased some of the tension for her.

"No. Bug and I are in cahoots."

I lifted an eyebrow. "But I thought he and I were besties."

I liked the way her golden curls bounced as she shook her head and how a slight dimple high up on her cheek appeared when she smiled hard.

"No. Me and the little guy bonded the first night. We had an agreement."

"Well, that's not fair," I said.

She leaned closer and brushed her lips softly over mine. She knew I couldn't move. I couldn't deepen the kiss or Bug would fall. "It's not supposed to be." She looked into my eyes and down to my mouth several times.

My mind was racing and my heart was pounding. "You do that a lot," I said.

"What do I do?"

"When you want me to kiss you, you stare at my lips."

She nodded. "You're not wrong."

"But I can't move." I pointed to Bug, who was alarmingly tangled in my hair. He was still purring, so I knew I was the only one close to panicking. "He's really in there."

"Do you need help?"

"Yes, please."

She leaned over me and carefully pulled strands of my hair from his grasp. I held her hips and tried not to moan as her breasts were inches from my face. She smelled like cinnamon and baked goods. I closed my eyes and tried not to hiss every time he clutched me to hang on. Once he realized he wasn't falling and Macey had a firm grasp, he released me. She snuggled him for a moment and put him in his bed with Lady.

"Where were we?"

"You wanted me to kiss you," I said.

"That's true. It's my reward for rescuing you," she said.

I cupped her face and brought it to mine for a soft kiss. I always felt alive when our lips touched. Our chemistry was one of my favorite things about us. "Let's give the kittens some quiet time," I said.

I almost tripped over her to get to my bed. I pulled her T-shirt off, followed quickly by my own. She unclasped her bra and tossed it while I ripped my sports bra off. Being naked with her was another one of my favorite things about us. I gently pushed her to the mattress and not so gently pulled her leggings off. My leggings came off fast and I crawled with her on the bed until I was over her, our breasts touching, her legs wrapped around mine, and my mouth inches from hers.

"Thank you for rescuing me," I said.

She brought my lips down to hers in a scorching kiss. I felt it everywhere. My rapid heartbeat pounded in my ears and made my entire body throb.

"I'm not naked." She groaned.

I quickly remedied that and ensured we were both completely naked before I climbed back into bed. I pushed her knees up and settled between them. She moaned at the contact and I moaned in response. She was wet and eager, but holding back. Her body was taut and it was just a matter of time before she flipped me and took control. Right now, she was letting me do whatever I wanted. I pushed my hands behind her knees and rolled my hips into her pussy. My knees rubbed against the soft sheets with every thrust. I didn't care. This felt too good to stop. I'd never used a strap-on before, but at this angle and her need, it would have been perfect. Instead, I slipped my hand between us and slid two fingers inside. She was tight at this angle, but her sounds of pleasure told me to keep doing it. She locked her arms under her knees to keep the angle while I held my weight over her on one hand. This way I was able to fuck her fast and hard.

"Oh, yes, oh, yes," she said.

I stopped to give my hand a rest and reached inside my nightstand to pull out my vibrator and lube. Not that she needed lube because the bed was soaked, but it just made it a more pleasurable and smooth experience. She lowered her legs so her feet were planted on the mattress. "This is only mine. I've only used it on me." I wanted to clear the air before we even got started. "Are you okay with this?" If she said no, I was going to use it on myself because I was so ready to explode.

She nodded. "Completely okay." Her voice was raspy and gave me chills.

I added lube and gently rubbed the tip up and down her slit. When I turned it on, her body jerked at the vibration.

"I can turn it off."

"Absolutely not." She licked her lips. Her quick, shallow breaths made her generous breasts heave, and I slid my free hand up her body to squeeze her nipple and rub my thumb over its hardness. The other hand had complete control of the vibrator that I moved up and down her slit.

"Go inside," she whispered.

I teased her and slid the tip in and pulled it out. She spread her legs wider apart and lifted her hips. After five times of just the tip, she moaned in pleasure and frustration.

"Fuck me."

It was a command that I felt in every part of my body. I slid the vibrator inside as far as she could take it. It wasn't large, but watching it slide in and out of her made me swollen with want. I wanted her to do the same to me. I could see how much pleasure I was giving her and wanted to preserve this moment forever. Her eyes fluttered shut. Her nipples were hard, chill bumps covered her body, her back was slightly arched, and she repeatedly licked her lips. Her hips bucked against my hand every time I slid it inside her. I sped the vibrator up, hoping that would increase the pleasure, and lifted it so it barely touched her clit. She clutched the arm that was keeping me balanced.

"Faster," she said.

My adrenaline was the only thing keeping me going. I was exhausted, sweaty, but exhilarated. I moved as fast as I could without slipping out of her, and when she came, she cried out and dug her fingers into me. She drew as much pleasure as she could with each aftershock. I was mesmerized and awestruck. I gathered her into my arms and pulled her on top of me. The bed was soaked and I didn't want her to think about it. I could feel her furious heartbeat as she laid her head on my chest. Maybe that was mine, but either way, that experience changed both of us. I pulled a blanket over us for comfort and waited for her body to relax against mine.

She placed her palm on my collarbone and rested her chin on it so she could look at me. "Just when I think things can't get any better, you surprise me."

I lazily played with a corkscrew curl. "Hashtag goals." I

smacked my palm to my forehead. "Scratch that. I'm nervous. I think we're only going to get better."

She laughed. "I don't know if my body can take better than that."

I'd thought of a million different ways to make love to Macey. This was only one. "Brace yourself because I'm going to spend every day we're together making it better." I didn't want it to sound only like sex, so I elaborated. "I'm not going to let work get in the way of us. I'm going to take you to more plays and we're going to spend time at the beach and I'm going to meet your family and we'll host barbecues for our friends."

"But what about the sex?"

I laughed and smiled when I felt her laugh rumble against my chest. "It's going to get better, too."

"I don't see how that's possible."

My ego inflated. I was never accused of being great in bed, but something about our chemistry and the fact that I'd fallen for Macey made loving her physically and emotionally the most natural and honest thing in my life. I closed my eyes and pulled Macey closer to me. I was happy and content.

❖

"Sawyer, wake up."

I groaned as those words made my life flash in front of my eyes. The real life with Dr. Macey and Lady and Bug and Healing Paws. I was hesitant to fully wake up even though I could feel sweat bead up as anxiety took hold of my conscious. I rolled over. I felt hands on my back.

"Baby, I can't find Bug."

My eyes flew open and I looked back at Macey.

"I wanted to let you sleep and feed them all by myself, but Bug has flown off somewhere," she said.

Even though her voice was full of concern, I smiled. This was my reality. "Let's go find him." I threw on my T-shirt and panties and turned on the flashlight on my phone. "I bet he's somewhere in the bedroom."

"Bug! Buggy Boy, where are you?" Macey's voice was more confident now that I was in the hunt. I looked under all the furniture but didn't find him. "How are you so calm?" she asked.

"Because logically he's in the house. They never stray too far. Let's check the closet. He's probably hanging out in a pair of shoes." I flipped the light on in my walk-in and got down on all fours to find that fluff ball. "Buggy, oh, Buggy. Where are you?" Thankfully, my closet was organized.

"Look. There he is," Macey said. We found him curled up in a pair of fluffy house slippers with giant unicorn heads on the toes. Macey took a photo of him before she scooped him up. "We've got you now, baby boy. You're safe. Come on. It's dinner time."

It would've been rude for me to point out that he wasn't scared. He was perfectly content in the closet. It was time to expand their environment. "What time is it?" I groaned.

"Go back to bed. I've got this," she said.

I fell back to sleep immediately but instantly woke up when I felt Macey's warm arm drape across my waist when she came back to bed. She snuggled flush against me, her breasts in my back and the tops of her thighs touching the back of mine. Her warm breath tickled the back of my neck.

"I love you, too," she said.

Chapter Twenty-two

I was going to have Tricks-for-Treats in the parking lot, but so many people RSVPed that I had to move the pet parade to the yard. Mom and Dad were in charge of the treat tent and Tamsyn and Arya were judging the costumes. I greeted everyone coming in and passed out toys with Healing Paws, our phone number, and a QR code to easily access our website and online store of pet food and supplements.

"I can't believe the turnout," Yara said.

"I'm stunned. I mean, I know a lot of people are here because they are curious and they want to show off their pet's costume, but this is amazing," I said. People were parking next door in the empty lot and along the curb all the way down the street. "How many VIP invitations did Lauren send out?"

"I'll check," Yara said.

She pulled her tablet out and scrolled. "Well, only about fifty."

"How did it get so big?" I was in awe.

"Social media. Somebody posted something and it spread."

"But we don't have the resources to handle this many people. We're going to run out of snacks," I said.

"Then we'll open more bags of snacks. We have a whole shelf of different, healthy snack options for dogs, cats, and rabbits," she said.

"I mean people snacks. Can you tell from here if we're running low?" I didn't plan for a big turnout. The grand prize was a fifty-dollar gift card to Healing Paws and a photo of the winner on our website.

My dad predicted my panic. "Honey, I'm going to run to the store and pick up more water and snacks. I'll be back in a flash," he said.

"Thanks, Dad. I appreciate it."

Macey texted that she and her family would be over at noon after feeding the babies and that she had a surprise for me. I texted her that I was close to panicking because so many people were there. She sent me a thumbs-up emoji and I sent her a puking one back.

See? You're already a big hit!

I slid my phone in my pocket. She was all about being positive and I needed somebody to full-on panic with me.

"Oh, more people. I'll go back inside," Yara said.

She squeezed my shoulder and left me sitting at a table between both places. They would have to talk to me if they wanted to participate in the costume contest. A lot of people were clients of Oliver Strong, but that didn't guarantee I would be their new vet. I smiled when I saw Princess and her owner. Princess was dressed as a ballerina complete with pink tutu and bejeweled bows in her hair. Her owner was wearing pink, and honestly, I wasn't sure if she was in costume or not.

"Thank you so much for coming," I said. I picked up Princess and scratched her chin. "Hello, gorgeous. We have a ton of treats for you up at the tent."

"Dr. Noel, I can't tell you how happy I am that you are away from that place. It really has gone downhill since you left." She lowered her voice in case anyone overheard. "I will definitely bring Princess here. Your services here are remarkable." She leafed through the trifold brochure I had printed.

"Honestly, I thought of you when I put the little playground in. I know how much you love it when Princess plays with her friends, so now you can come up and hang out whenever it's available." I had a tiny bit of regret after I told her only because she would show up tomorrow, opening day, and try to not be in the way but completely be in the way. "There's a picnic table and plenty of chairs. It'll give you an opportunity to meet other owners who love their pets as much as you love Princess." I told her to be sure to visit the tent where there were homemade treats for Princess and where she could enter Princess in the costume contest, then excused myself.

My heart jumped when I recognized Macey's car pull into the parking lot next door. I knew her family was coming up to see the place and meet me. It wasn't the ideal way to meet for the first time, but we weren't sure what my schedule was going to be like over the next two months. When she suggested it, a quick meet-and-greet at my new business sounded fast and stressless, but now it felt like the exact opposite. What was I thinking? Macey swore it would be casual and carefree, but I wanted to make a good first impression and not smell like dog and hay.

I had no time to check my appearance, fix my hair, or get mentally prepared for such a big step in our relationship even though I knew she was bringing them. I waved and smiled and pretended my heart hadn't tried to leap out of my chest or that my stomach wasn't trying to rid itself of the last five pieces of candy. When two goldendoodles jumped out the back of Macey's parents' car, I gasped. They were gorgeous and I couldn't wait to meet them. Macey walked a few paces in front of her parents and right into my arms.

"Hi," I said. She felt so good pressed against me.

"Hi. My parents just happen to be in the market for a new veterinarian and I told them about this really awesome new place that just opened. So they brought Booth and Bones."

I knew I was going to love her parents just because of the dogs' names. Anyone who named their pets after television shows were going to be awesome. "That's amazing. Thank you." My heart sped up the closer they got to me. I didn't know who to greet first as the goldendoodles bounced over to me. I said a quick hello to the *Bones* characters and stood up straight when Macey introduced me for the first time.

"These are my parents, Royce and Mary Burr," she said.

Sweat popped out everywhere and I hoped nobody noticed. "Hi, I'm Sawyer Noel. It's nice to meet you. I've heard so much about you." I shook both their hands and gave the dogs each a peanut butter bone cookie that Arya made. They gobbled them up. Booth poked my leg with his snout, demanding another. I obliged. I was under scrutiny of both people and canines.

"Can you please take this up to the tent?" Macey handed a box to her parents, promptly dismissing them.

"We'll talk later, Sawyer," Mary said.

"I know I said I wasn't sure if the rest of my family was coming or not, but they decided to. I hope that's okay," Macey said after her parents left us alone.

"I think it's great. When are they getting here?" I asked.

Macey looked at her watch. "Any time. They were behind me, but Alyssa had to stop for gas."

Five minutes later, I met her brothers and sisters-in-law, nieces and nephews. I almost cried when I met Aunt Abby because of the impact she had on Macey's life. She was kind and hugged me with one arm. The other arm was leaning on a quad cane.

"Hi, Sawyer," she said.

"Hi, Aunt Abby." She was Aunt Abby to me. "Welcome to my new business."

"It's so big. And all the animals are just so cute. I can't wait to see the contest," she said.

Macey kissed me swiftly. "I'll get her settled and will be right back."

I was overwhelmed by everything. My family, Macey's family, all the people who came out to support my new business. It was a lot. When my dad returned with a wagon of water and boxes of pastries, I lost it.

"What's wrong, sweetie?" He gathered me into a hug.

I always felt safe in his arms. I hadn't cried on his shoulder in a really long time, but I really needed his support. "Everything's perfect."

He chuckled and stroked my hair. "Then why are you crying?"

I sniffled and dropped my arms. "It's so much. So much has changed in six months."

He brushed away a few tears. "I can't believe how much you were able to get done. I mean I can because you're my daughter, but it's been an amazing ride, hasn't it?"

I knew he wasn't trying to take credit for my accomplishments, so I let it slide. I did it because of me. Because I had a second chance to make the right choice in my life. I was taking care of me. And in the process, I met a wonderful woman.

"Are you sure you're okay? Your mother is waving me over and you know I don't want to upset her," he said.

I nodded. "Thanks, Dad. I'm going to pop inside and make sure I still look presentable."

He cupped my face with his giant hands. "You'll always be beautiful."

I checked out my reflection in the bathroom mirror. My nose was slightly red, but that was about it. I dried my happy tears and returned to my post.

"Where'd you go?" Macey pulled me into a hug, sensing that I needed strength.

"I had to make sure I looked okay. Meeting your entire family, while incredibly exciting, was also a tiny bit terrifying," I said. I held up my finger and thumb with a sliver of space between them. "Tiny bit."

"They love you already. My mom keeps talking about how beautiful you are, and Aunt Abby has already adopted you into the family."

"They're very nice. And Aunt Abby? I love her. She's so nice." I couldn't stop saying nice, but they all were.

"She loves that you call her Aunt Abby already," Macey said. She thumbed behind her. "Also, I brought over more all things pumpkin. Tamsyn said people weren't shy about eating."

"I thought for sure people would just stop in, say hello, and then leave. Macey, nobody has left. This place is packed."

She squeezed my hand. "I'm so proud of you. When do you think you can leave your post and hang out with all your new clients, including my family who has already signed up for yearly check-ups?" She pointed at Yara who was filling out new patient forms on her tablet. Somehow Yara got around me.

"Then who's at the front desk?"

"Lauren. You walked right by her," Macey said.

I shook my head. "It's been a day." I held my finger up and peeked in the front door. "Thanks, Lauren. I didn't even see you there."

She shooed me out. "Go, have fun. Talk to your new clients. I've got this."

I blew her a kiss and followed Macey to the yard where so many animals dressed in costumes were hanging out with their owners. Tamsyn and Arya were judging and mostly throwing perfect scores around. When two o'clock rolled around and we had to announce the winner, it was a three-way-tie between an adorable Rottweiler in a tutu, a cat named Joker dressed as a court jester, and a ferret dressed as a hot dog called Boo-boo. I was super impressed with Arya's hamster, Harry, who strutted around in his cage wearing the cutest blue Hawaiian shirt and didn't try to take it off.

"How is she able to get him to keep that on?" I asked Tamsyn.

"I feel like they are telepathically connected somehow. It's cute but also weird," she said.

Tamsyn passed out gift cards to the winners and announced that Healing Paws was closing so everyone could go home and enjoy Halloween. By three, everything was clean, locked up, and the parking lot empty. I was exhausted.

"Let's go home. I'm sure the babies are ready to eat. I know I am," Macey said.

"I'm going to order a pizza for pickup on the way." I was very aware that we were both talking about going home, but it meant the same place.

"You go home with the babies and relax. I'll pick up the pizza. It's been a long and exciting day for you," she said. She kissed me and slipped into her coupe.

It took me twenty minutes to pack up Lady and Bug, who were already getting used to my office, and head home. They were ready to eat the minute their paws hit the kitchen tile. I finished feeding them right when Macey walked in with the pizza. She dropped it on the counter and reached for Lady.

"Hello, Ladyboo. Did you miss us?"

"Smitten by a kitten," I said. I moved closer so she could say hi to Bug, too.

"Who would've thought?" she asked.

I pointed to myself. "I knew. And you didn't believe me."

"Well, I believe you now," she said. She dumped out their toy box in the living room, where they could play with toys while we ate.

"Maybe it's just me, but this is the best pizza I've ever had," It was my hunger talking and my adrenaline waning.

"It's great, but you haven't really eaten today. You were too excited this morning and you had maybe one pumpkin cheesecake bar. You need energy," Macey said.

She took a bite of pizza, wiped her mouth, and gave a recap of the day. Her sweet, calming voice rose and fell with each exciting moment she witnessed. She told me about how several of my clients were discussing meeting up this week in the play park and how everyone thought it was a great idea. She was impressed with Arya because she helped a new customer by showing him how to scan the QR code to quickly place online orders. Even though I was exhausted, it was hard not to feel a rush at her words. I had everything. A job I loved, a support group who believed in me, and the perfect girlfriend. Macey's brows quirked.

"Are you listening to me? You have that far-off, dreamy look on your face," she said.

I smiled. "I heard every word you said. It's just so unbelievable. Look at my life today and how different it was six months ago. All because of a car wreck." I was proud, overwhelmed, and emotionally drained. I wanted to cry, but I was too tired.

"You've come a long way and it wasn't easy at all." She held my hand. "You overcame so much in such a short time. It's admirable," she said.

I kissed her softly and touched her cheek. I stared into her eyes, wanting to tell her just how much I loved her and how I loved my life so much more with her in it, but words weren't enough. I was going to have to spend the rest of my life showing her. "All of my dreams finally came true."

EPILOGUE

"I t's not too late," I said.

I stood in Macey's door with an animal carrier and my messenger bag. She leaned against the doorframe for a moment as though she was contemplating my statement and then squealed and threw her arms around my neck.

"It's too late," she said. She kissed my cheek and squeezed me hard. "You're officially stuck here with me. Forever."

"Forever, huh?" I asked. I handed her the carrier. She put it on the floor and opened the door. Bug pounced out.

"Forever, yes." She looked at me. "You're okay with this move, right?"

I played with one of her loose curls and wrapped it around my finger. "I'm perfectly okay. I'm exactly where I want to be."

I had officially moved in with Macey. We joked around over New Year's Eve, but suddenly it wasn't funny and I put my place on the market in the spring. Healing Paws was flourishing. I hired two additional veterinarians and three technicians. I gave myself time off. Whenever Macey could take time off, we spent the day or weekend together. "Lady and Bug will be happy to only have one house." Juggling them between the two places wasn't easy. Bug didn't like to travel and was vocal about it. Sadly, they weren't ready to be office cats. They were my last load from the townhouse.

"This is it, buddy. No more commuting. This is your home," Macey said. She freed Lady and pulled me in her arms. "This is your home, too, so if there's something you don't like or want to change, say something. It's a newish house, but I want you to be comfortable here, too."

Her house was amazing. I couldn't imagine changing anything about it. "No, it's gorgeous. Don't change a single thing."

"I love you," she said.

"I love you, too," I said.

Her fingers brushed across my chest and landed on my collarbone. She sighed regrettably. "As nice as it would be to show you just how much I do love you, we need to get to Tamsyn's. The barbecue starts in half an hour. We have enough time to change and head that way," Macey said.

"By we, you mean me, right?" I asked. When Macey smiled, she lit up the whole room. It was hard to be in a bad mood when she was so happy.

"You are sexy, and beautiful, and also full of kitten hair. At least change your clothes." She wrinkled her nose adorably to soften the blow.

"Okay, I'm going to change. I'll be right down." I jogged up the stairs and stripped for a quick shower. I grabbed fresh clothes and was downstairs in twenty minutes. "We'll only be a few minutes late. They aren't going to be mad. Tamsyn knows this is a big day for us."

"I'll drive," she said.

She got no argument from me. We pulled up and Tamsyn burst out of the front door with her arms wide open, ready to hug us both.

"Is it official?" she yelled.

We both nodded.

"Yes! Best day ever! Congratulations," she said.

She put her arm around my shoulders and walked me into the house. "Now don't fuck it up." She said it loud enough for Macey to hear and was rewarded with a sweet laugh. This moment made my heart jump. I was finally getting somewhere in life. I wasn't going through the motions anymore.

"Did you bring the kittens?" Arya gave us hugs and looked at us expectantly.

I held my palms out to show I wasn't hiding them. "No, they are getting used to their forever home, but you can come over tomorrow and play with them if you want."

"I can invite Ana and Lee to come over and we can watch a movie if you want." Macey's nieces were a couple of years older than Arya, but they all played well together.

"And we can play with the kittens!" Arya said.

I looked at Tamsyn and smiled. It was just a matter of time before they caved. I fully supported Arya having a kitten. She was so good with Harry, and most kids her age got bored with their pets, but not Arya. She was almost magical with animals. I told her she always would have a job at Healing Paws whenever she was ready.

"Congratulations to our best friends for finding love and doing something about it," Lauren said.

"Thank you for being such wonderful friends to Sawyer and for accepting me into your circle. I love you all," Macey said.

I was getting emotional seeing my friends bond with Macey. They had never approved of anyone I've dated before, and their approval made my heart soar.

"All of my dreams came true," I said. I knew that I was saying and thinking that a lot, but it was the biggest truth in my heart.

Tamsyn nudged me. "Here's to chasing your dreams but finally living the real ones."

About the Author

Multi-award-winning author Kris Bryant was born in Tacoma, WA, but has lived all over the world and now considers Kansas City her home. She received her BA in English from the University of Missouri and spends a lot of her time buried in books. She enjoys binge-watching TV, photography, kayaking, and spending time with her internet famous pooch, Molly.

Her first novel, *Jolt*, was a Lambda Literary Finalist. *Forget Me Not* was selected by the American Library Association's 2018 Over the Rainbow book list. *Breakthrough* won a 2019 Goldie for Contemporary Romance. *Listen* won a 2020 Goldie for Contemporary Romance. *Temptation* won a 2021 Goldie for Contemporary Romance. And writing under Brit Ryder, *Not Guilty* won a 2022 Goldie for Erotic Romance. Kris can be reached at krisbryantbooks@gmail.com or www.krisbryant.net, @krisbryant14.

Books Available From Bold Strokes Books

Appalachian Awakening by Nance Sparks. The more Amber's and Leslie's paths cross, the more this hike of a lifetime begins to look like a love of a lifetime. (978-1-63679-527-0)

Dreamer by Kris Bryant. When life seems to be too good to be true and love is within reach, Sawyer and Macey discover the truth about the town of Ladybug Junction, and the cold light of reality tests the hearts of these dreamers. (978-1-63679-378-8)

Eyes on Her by Eden Darry. When increasingly violent acts of sabotage threaten to derail the opening of her glamping business, Callie Pope is sure her ex, Jules, has something to do with it. But Jules is dead…isn't she? (978-1-63679-214-9)

Letters from Sarah by Joy Argento. A simple mistake brought them together, but Sarah must release past love to create a future with Lindsey she never dreamed possible. (978-1-63679-509-6)

Lost in the Wild by Kadyan. When their plane crash-lands, Allison and Mike face hunger, cold, a terrifying encounter with a bear, and feelings for each other neither expects. (978-1-63679-545-4)

Not Just Friends by Jordan Meadows. A tragedy leaves Jen struggling to figure out who she is and what is important to her. (978-1-63679-517-1)

Of Auras and Shadows by Jennifer Karter. Eryn and Rina's unexpected love may be exactly what the Community needs to heal the rot that comes not from the fetid Dark Lands that surround the Community but from within. (978-1-63679-541-6)

The Secret Duchess by Jane Walsh. A determined widow defies a duke and falls in love with a fashionable spinster in a fight for her rightful home. (978-1-63679-519-5)

Winter's Spell by Ursula Klein. When former college roommates reunite at a wedding in Provincetown, sparks fly, but can they find true love when evil sirens and trickster mermaids get in the way? (978-1-63679-503-4)

Coasting and Crashing by Ana Hartnett. Life comes easy to Emma Wilson until Lake Palmer shows up at Alder University and derails her every plan. (978-1-63679-511-9)

Every Beat of Her Heart by KC Richardson. Piper and Gillian have their own fears about falling in love, but will they be able to overcome those feelings once they learn each other's secrets? (978-1-63679-515-7)

Fire in the Sky by Radclyffe and Julie Cannon. Two women from different worlds have nothing in common and every reason to wish they'd never met—except for the attraction neither can deny. (978-1-63679-561-4)

Grave Consequences by Sandra Barret. A decade after necromancy became licensed and legalized, can Tamar and Maddy overcome the lingering prejudice against their kind and their growing attraction to each other to uncover a plot that threatens both their lives? (978-1-63679-467-9)

Haunted by Myth by Barbara Ann Wright. When ghost-hunter Chloe seeks an answer to the current spectral epidemic, all clues point to one very famous face: Helen of Troy, whose motives are more complicated than history suggests and whose charms few can resist. (978-1-63679-461-7)

Invisible by Anna Larner. When medical school dropout Phoebe Frink falls for the shy costume shop assistant Violet Unwin, everything about their love feels certain, but can the same be said about their future? (978-1-63679-469-3)

Like They Do in the Movies by Nan Campbell. Celebrity gossip writer Fran Underhill becomes Chelsea Cartwright's personal assistant with the aim of taking the popular actress down, but neither of them anticipates the clash of their attraction. (978-1-63679-525-6)

Limelight by Gun Brooke. Liberty Bell and Palmer Elliston loathe each other. They clash every week on the hottest new TV show, until Liberty starts to sing and the impossible happens. (978-1-63679-192-0)

BOLDSTROKESBOOKS.COM

Looking for your next great read?

Visit BOLDSTROKESBOOKS.COM
to browse our entire catalog of paperbacks, ebooks,
and audiobooks.

Want the first word on what's new?
Visit our website for event info,
author interviews, and blogs.

Subscribe to our free newsletter for sneak peeks,
new releases, plus first notice of promos
and daily bargains.

SIGN UP AT
BOLDSTROKESBOOKS.COM/signup

Bold Strokes Books
Quality and Diversity in LGBTQ Literature

*Bold Strokes Books is an award-winning publisher
committed to quality and diversity in LGBTQ fiction.*